Caught in the web of the
vampire spiders are ...
The Lair
The Ghost
of
Lady Withers
Lord Withers'
Skeleton
Dr Clinton
'talking spider'
Lord Withers' Poot
D0865439

Susan Gates says …

I got the idea for this story in a toilet. Inside the ladies' toilet, to be exact, on the platform of a steam railway station. Those toilets were beautifully looked after. They even had vases of flowers. The Visitors' Book was full of nice comments: 'These toilets sparkle!' There was only one mean comment. It was written in nasty, spiky handwriting, and it said, 'What about the cobweb?' Somehow cleaning, spiders and handwriting got all mixed up in my mind and Invasion of the Vampire Spiders *was born!*

Some other books by Susan Gates

ATTACK OF THE TENTACLED TERROR

KILLER MUSHROOMS ATE MY GRAN

NIGHT OF THE HAUNTED TROUSERS

REVENGE OF THE TOFFEE MONSTER

Susan Gates

Invasion of the Vampire Spiders

Illustrated by Tony Blundell

PUFFIN BOOKS

PUFFIN BOOKS

Penguin Books Ltd, 80 Strand, London WC2R 0RL, England
Penguin Putnam Inc., 375 Hudson Street, New York, New York 10014, USA
Penguin Books Australia Ltd, 250 Camberwell Road, Camberwell,
Victoria 3124, Australia
Penguin Books Canada Ltd, 10 Alcorn Avenue, Toronto, Ontario, Canada M4V 3B2
Penguin Books India (P) Ltd, 11 Community Centre, Panchsheel Park,
New Delhi – 110 017, India
Penguin Books (NZ) Ltd, Cnr Rosedale and Airborne Roads, Albany,
Auckland, New Zealand
Penguin Books (South Africa) (Pty) Ltd, 24 Sturdee Avenue, Rosebank 2196, South Africa

On the World Wide Web at: www.penguin.com

Penguin Books Ltd, Registered Offices: 80 Strand, London WC2R 0RL, England

First published 2001
1

Set in Baskerville MT

Made and printed in England by Clays Ltd, St Ives plc

British Library Cataloguing in Publication Data
A CIP catalogue record for this book is available from the British Library

ISBN 0–141–31074–X

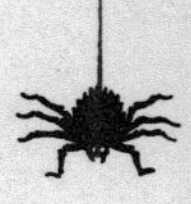

Chapter One

Finn swallowed a spider.

'Yurgh!' He made horrid choking sounds in his throat. He spat into his hand and inspected the poor, broken body. Then he threw down his spider-hunter's pooter.

'Stupid thing!'

He booted the pooter down the hill. He was really upset. It had made him kill a spider, and that was the last thing he wanted to do. Finn was a big fan of arachnids. He thought they were the most perfect, the most fascinating creatures on the planet. He loved creepy crawlies of all kinds. He was the only kid in his class who looked forward to catching head lice.

He'd made the pooter from a diagram in a book for spider enthusiasts. It was a small glass tube with two open ends. Only, on one end was fixed a rubber pipe.

The theory was – you spotted your spider, then sucked him gently through the rubber pipe into the glass tube and bunged in a cork before he could run away.

'Only I can't suck gently!' wailed Finn.

He kept sucking too hard, so the spider shot through the glass tube, up the rubber tube and into his mouth. He'd eaten eight today already.

'I'm a spider murderer,' thought Finn sadly.

That put him into the category of people he most despised. Finn had a simple view of the world. He divided it into two groups. The people who swilled spiders down the plughole – they were enemies. And the people who didn't – they were friends.

Finn decided to give up trying to catch spiders. He'd got a big collection in his bedroom anyway, living in glass tanks and shoe boxes with mesh on the top. His mum was always complaining.

'They give me the creeps. Why don't you get some nice, furry pets?'

'My tarantula's nice and furry,' Finn objected.

'Yes, but it's not *cuddly*, is it? Not like a rabbit or a guinea pig.'

Finn had dark suspicions about his mum. He'd once caught her brushing a cobweb from the car steering wheel. And when he'd protested, 'Mum! That is some poor spider's *home*! Plus, it's a work *of art*,' she'd just said, 'Too bad! I've got to drive to the shops. It shouldn't have built it there.'

'Nobody gives spiders enough respect,' sighed Finn.

They would if they knew more about them. If they knew, for instance, that spiders walked the earth long before dinosaurs; that they'd been around for 250 million years; that some spiders could *smell* through their feet.

Finn sprawled in the grass and watched them. This high, breezy moorland was a perfect playground for spiders.

There wasn't much else to see: only miles of heather, some big grey rocks, and their own house that had once been a school. Dad said there used to be a village near by. But all that was left of it now were heaps of stones.

There was just one other house. You could see it from here. It was on a craggy ridge just opposite. It was called The Lair – a weird jumble of towers and battlements, half fortress, half fairy-tale castle.

'I wonder who lives there,' thought Finn idly.

He didn't know the neighbours yet. Finn and his mum and dad and big sister, Phoebe, had only moved to the moors two weeks ago. The Lair was a strange place, wild and grand and sinister.

You'd need pots of cash to live there, thought Finn.

Then he stopped thinking. He'd felt the grass stems shiver. Spiders!

Finn held his breath. Right in front of his nose, some baby spiders were leaving their nest for the first time. Each one was as small as a full stop. Yet they were hurling themselves, on flimsy silken threads, out into the big wide world.

'Be safe,' whispered Finn to the brave little bungee jumpers. It was scary out there for spiderlings. Frogs, toads, birds, wasps, shrews – Finn hated to think of all the things that could gobble them up. Including spider hunters with homemade pooters.

'That pooter was useless!' he thought angrily.

A furry caterpillar shimmied across the track. Finn rested his face on the mud so he had a bug's eye view. Something loomed up behind the caterpillar. At first it was fuzzy, not in focus. Finn blinked. Then he saw it was a large brown hiking boot.

'Hey!' he said hotly. 'Don't squash my caterpillar.'

'What are you doing down there, young man?' came the brisk question from somewhere above him.

Finn's gaze went up and up from the boots. Past the red woollen knee socks, the tweedy pleated skirt, the chunky cardie, to a broad, pale freckly face. What strange hair! It frizzed out like an orange dandelion clock. The face wore big black mirror shades – like tough American motorcycle cops in films.

Finn gulped.

'I am Miss Burgess,' the face announced, in a booming voice that made the tiny spiderlings scoot for safety. 'And I have come for the contents of my cupboard.'

Finn scrambled to his feet. He felt like he

should be standing to attention. Even saluting! But he couldn't. His body didn't know how to stand up straight. It just naturally sagged into a slouch.

I wish I could see her eyes, thought Finn uncomfortably. But they were hidden behind those menacing shades. All he could see was himself, reflected twice in their glittering lenses.

'You were daydreaming,' said Miss Burgess. It sounded like something she disapproved of.

'*Err, err*,' gabbled Finn guiltily. She made him feel like he ought to apologize. He said the first thing that came into his head. 'I was daydreaming about being brought up by spiders. You hear a lot about lost kids in the jungle being raised by wolves, even by gorillas. But do you ever hear of them being brought up by spiders? No! And I don't understand it because spiders make excellent parents. So long as your mum doesn't eat your dad, that is –'

Miss Burgess regarded the small boy before her with serious concern. Was he quite right in the head? The words rushing out of his mouth made no sense at all. And why couldn't he stand up straight? Why was he jiggling about like that?

'Do you need the toilet?' she asked Finn sternly, peering at him over her sunglasses.

Finn heard her but thought, Naa! She can't have said what she just said. He decided his ears were playing tricks. Now he could see her eyes she didn't look so threatening. They were palest watery blue, like a summer sky after rain.

She repeated her question, more slowly and clearly this time. 'Do – you – want – a – wee-wee?'

Oh no! thought Finn, panicking all over again. I did hear her right first time! He was shocked and deeply embarrassed. What's she asking me that for? No one had asked him those kinds of questions for years. Not since he was potty trained. Except for that time he'd had an accident on the fairground big wheel. The people in the seats below were very upset. But he preferred to forget about that.

Miss Burgess clicked her tongue in frustration. '*Tsk, tsk, tsk.* There I go again! Just take no notice. I've spent a lifetime teaching tiny tots. Old habits die hard. Once a teacher always a teacher. I'm probably shouting rather loudly now, aren't I? And repeating myself a lot?'

'*Err*, no,' mumbled Finn, shaking his head to stop his ears ringing.

He longed for her to stop pestering him so he could get back to his spiders. It was nice and quiet, studying spiders.

'Because I do tend to say things twice!' bellowed Miss Burgess as if she was breaking up a schoolyard fight. She took off her specs and blinked. 'Weak eyes,' she explained.

A sudden thought struck Finn. 'Do you live in The Lair?' he asked her. If she didn't, he couldn't understand where she'd sprung from. The nearest town was five miles away.

Miss Burgess gave a hearty guffaw. '*Haw! Haw!*' Three fields away a flock of crows heard her. They whirled with startled '*Caws!*' into the sky.

'My dear boy!' she said, patting him on the head as if he was a puppy. 'What a good joke! No, I don't live there. You won't find many ex-teachers like me living in castles!'

Finn squirmed. He hated his hair being touched. Even his own mum didn't do that.

He gritted his teeth. Who was this irritating person? She'd spoiled his peaceful spider watching. She'd just ruined his spiky hairstyle. He'd spent ages in the bathroom that morning gelling it into place.

At that moment he'd have bet you anything, anything you liked, that Miss Burgess was the kind of villain who'd give a cruel laugh – before flushing a poor innocent spider down the drain.

Miss Burgess settled her shades on her nose. She grasped her hiking stick.

That's strange, thought Finn. She was the sort of person you'd expect to have some kind of gnarled and knobbly wooden stick. But this one was sleek, silver metal.

She saw Finn looking at it.

She turned the stick upside down. It folded up into her hand like a telescope. It had become a tea cup!

'It's a state-of-the-art, dual-purpose, collapsible titanium hiking stick and tea cup,' said Miss Burgess. 'Very lightweight. Here, feel.'

She tipped the little cup into Finn's hand.

'Wow!' said Finn, despite himself. It felt very

fragile. If he closed his fist he might crunch it up like an eggshell.

'It's very strong,' said Miss Burgess, as if reading his mind. 'Nothing will break that. If I fall down a cliff when hiking I'll be smashed to bits. But my titanium stick won't have a mark on it.'

'Oh,' said Finn, looking baffled. 'Is that good?'

He gave back the stick. With a casual twist of her wrist, Miss Burgess flicked it out to its full length.

'Ready to go,' she said.

She waved her state-of-the-art stick at the Old School, where Finn lived. 'Forward!' she cried, crushing some spiderlings under her big boots.

Finn gasped with shock. He forgot about her fascinating stick. Now he hated Miss Burgess to his very bones.

'You spider murderer!' murmured Finn grimly.

He watched her trampling feet and swinging skirt disappear down to the house. He was glad she'd gone.

I get enough of teachers at school, he

thought, without meeting them in my summer holidays when I'm trying to relax.

Then suddenly she turned round. She started to walk back towards him! Her shades were scary sparkling discs. He cringed. Oh no, he thought. What's she want now?

'Actually,' she roared at him in a voice loud enough to scatter the sheep, 'if you're interested in The Lair – it's been empty for ages. But my nephew Dr Clinton C. Clinton is moving in this very day.'

'Not Dr Clinton C. Clinton, the famous spider psychologist?'

'I see you've heard of him,' said Miss Burgess.

'Heard of him?' Finn could hardly believe his luck. 'He's a star. A mega star!'

'I hear he's quite famous,' added Miss Burgess briskly. She didn't sound very impressed. 'Some television programme, I believe. I've never seen it myself. I don't approve of television. It rots children's brains.'

Instantly Finn forgave her for everything. For having big, spider-crushing plates of meat. And even for not liking telly. She'd just given him the best bit of news he'd ever had in his entire life! He hugged himself in sheer joy.

'*Wow!*' he gasped. He was thrilled to bits. '*Wow!* Dr Clinton C. Clinton, my hero! Coming to live next door to *me*!'

There was a sudden tinkle of breaking glass.

Oh no, she's stepped on my pooter! thought Finn.

'It's all right,' he assured her hastily. 'It was only my pooter, for catching spiders. It didn't work anyway.'

Miss Burgess didn't look puzzled, as anyone might. She bent down and poked at the broken pooter with her hiking stick.

'You need ladies' tights!' she declared. Her booming voice echoed round the hill tops. '*Ladies' tights! Ladies' tights!*'

Aaargh! thought Finn.

He felt himself shrivelling up, like a slug drenched with salt. He felt an urgent need to escape. Was this the most embarrassing person in the world? The universe? How was she related to someone as super cool as Dr Clinton C. Clinton?

'You cut up the tights,' she explained, 'and put a tiny piece between the glass tube and the rubber one. You can suck air through it. But not your spider. No danger of swallowing him. See? He's quite safe.'

'Cool!' Finn's face was suddenly bright with relief and understanding. 'Thanks,' he added gratefully. 'Thanks!'

He watched her stride away again.

That's a good idea, he thought. He couldn't understand why he hadn't thought of it first. He was changing his mind about Miss Burgess. Someone who knew about pooters couldn't be all bad. And, apart from that, she was Dr Clinton's auntie, so she deserved some kind of respect.

He remembered what she'd said, right at the start of their meeting. 'I wonder,' he asked himself, 'what's in her cupboard?'

Then he forgot her. He'd just spotted something really exciting. A motorbike was snarling up the twisty road to The Lair.

'That's *him*. On his metallic-blue Harley Davidson!'

Finn clasped his hands together, entranced.

'I can't believe it!' he breathed. 'Clinton C. Clinton rocks! And he's going to be my new neighbour.'

Suddenly, life seemed full of rainbows. The

world's top expert in spider behaviour moving in next to him, the world's biggest spider fan.

It's got to be fate, Finn decided.

Dr Clinton was on a TV show called *Pets with Problems*. He sorted out spiders. Is your pet tarantula sulking in a corner? Consult Clinton C. Clinton. Has your wolf spider lost interest in life? Dr Clinton will tell you why.

And he always could. It was almost spooky. He was brilliant at dealing with stressed-out spiders. As if he could read their minds.

His show was a big hit. Parents complained that their kids kept pestering them for pet spiders. But Finn thought it was great. It was about time spiders got popular. Spiders got a very bad press. When did you last hear *good* news about them? But Dr Clinton showed that spiders had feelings, just like the rest of us. 'Spiders Need Friends Too' was his catchphrase. Now kids thought twice before stomping on them or flushing them down the loo.

At least, some kids did.

In Finn's mind, Dr Clinton was the best ambassador for arachnids ever. He was cool. I mean really cool, thought Finn.

The only *uncool* thing he did was wear too-tight jeans on TV. But Finn could forgive him for that. It's a big mistake, he reasoned, to wear baggy pants when handling shy or upset spiders. It's practically inviting them to run up your trouser leg.

I wonder if he'll take a peek at my zebra spider?

Finn's zebra spider had been worrying him for weeks. She wasn't her usual happy self.

I'll just stroll over there in the morning and say 'Hi!', Finn decided. And me and Dr Clinton can have a good long chat about spiders.

Chapter Two

Phoebe had found someone's school timetable. It had a name at the top, *Ruby Dove,* and a date, *Christmas Term 1880.* Ruby Dove had written it out in beautiful handwriting. But it was the weirdest school timetable Phoebe had ever seen. These were Monday's lessons:

MONDAY
6.00 a.m. to 9.00 a.m. Dusting
Breakfast
9.30 a.m. to 12.30 p.m. Polishing
Lunch
1.00 p.m. to 4.00 p.m. Scrubbing
4.00 p.m. to 6.30 p.m. Laundry
Supper
Bed

And all the days were exactly the same. Except sometimes she had polishing before dusting. And sometimes she did laundry before scrubbing. And on Wednesdays, whoopee, she did three hours of mopping!

'This must be some kind of joke!' Phoebe told herself.

It looked genuine though. It was yellow and crinkly like paper a hundred years old.

She'd been rummaging around in the attic of the Old School. Just for something to do. She'd been in a funny mood ever since they'd moved house to live on the moors. She hardly knew who she was. She'd left all her friends behind. All the familiar places she'd known all her life. She'd left her old school behind. And until she started her new school in September she felt really strange. As if she was in limbo. Just waiting for things to happen.

She frowned at Ruby Dove's timetable. What kind of a useless school is this, she was thinking, where you have to do dusting for three hours before breakfast?

And she was still puzzling about it when Miss Burgess rang at the Old School door.

At first Phoebe ignored her. She thought, Why doesn't Dad answer it? But when she looked out the attic window she could see Dad. He was in their massive, jungly garden, at the spooky end, hacking down those dark rhododendron bushes. And, up on the sunlit moors, she could see Finn, spider watching. In a little world of his own, as usual.

Phoebe knew Mum was at work. She was the only one in the house. But she still let the doorbell ring.

Downstairs, Miss Burgess stood with her finger pressed on the bell. She knew Phoebe was in. Phoebe's dad had just told her.

Where is this child? thought Miss Burgess. In her day, children answered doorbells pretty smartish.

Up in the attic, Phoebe sighed. Slowly, she began trudging down the stairs. She had Ruby Dove's school timetable in her hand. She thought that whoever was ringing would have gone by the time she got there.

Fat chance. Miss Burgess was ready to ring until doomsday. She wanted what was in her cupboard and she wasn't about to be thwarted by children.

At last the door to the Old School opened a crack. Miss Burgess took off her shades.

Phoebe's suspicious eyes peered out at her: 'Yep?'

Miss Burgess was not put off. *'Ahem,'* she said, sticking her hiking boot in the door so Phoebe couldn't close it. 'I used to teach here, many, many moons ago. I inadvertently left some personal belongings in my classroom cupboard. I have your father's permission to collect them.'

Reluctantly, Phoebe opened the door a crack. She'd summed up Miss Burgess in five seconds flat. Old-fashioned teacher type, not child-friendly. In other words, strict old bat.

I bet she used to teach dusting, thought Phoebe. There's no way I'm letting her through this door.

But Miss Burgess was already muscling her way in. She looked around, and her face softened. Nothing had changed. There were still six tiny toilets in the cloakroom and a forest of iron coat pegs.

'I haven't been in here since it closed,' she explained. 'I was glad when I heard someone had moved in. This place has been locked up for twenty years. At least now I can get to my cupboard.'

She strode forward without being invited.

She's a freaky-looking person, thought Phoebe uneasily. With that frizzy orange clown's hair and strange, pale blue eyes.

'Did you really teach dusting?' She couldn't imagine Miss Burgess flicking a feather duster around.

But Miss Burgess wasn't listening. She was clumping into the first classroom. She greeted her long-lost cupboard with a loud cry. 'It's here!'

Why's she shouting like that? thought Phoebe. I'm not deaf.

'My cupboard is still in its former position!' explained Miss Burgess in an even more ear-splitting bellow, just in case Phoebe hadn't been paying attention the first time.

Miss Burgess took a key out her cardie pocket. Phoebe's dad had meant to find a key for that cupboard and clear it out. He just hadn't got round to it yet.

After all this time, the lock was rusty. With strong fingers, Miss Burgess wrenched the key round.

'This is my Nature Cupboard,' Miss Burgess told Phoebe, opening the door. 'At the end of each day I'd say, "Let's look in my Nature Cupboard!" The children would sit very quiet, with their hands on their heads. And then I'd get out one of my marvels!'

Miss Burgess pulled something out of her cupboard. It was brown and crusty and pizza-shaped.

'Yuk!' said Phoebe. 'What's that?'

'It's a dried-out cake of water buffalo dung, of course,' announced Miss Burgess. 'They use it for fuel in the Philippines. Now, isn't that fascinating? You can ask me questions, if you like. As long as they're sensible.'

Phoebe struggled hard to think of a single sensible question. Finn should have been here. He was an expert on animal droppings. He even had a book to identify them called, *Splat! What Was That?*

Miss Burgess waited. And waited. She'd expected a bit more wonderment.

'I suppose there wouldn't be time,' she said, shaking her head sadly, 'to squeeze buffalo dung into today's school syllabus.'

Thank goodness, thought Phoebe gratefully.

But she didn't say it out loud. Miss Burgess was six foot two in her hiking socks. She looked like she did tag wrestling as a hobby.

'We don't learn about dusting now either,' said Phoebe, sounding as sneery as she dared. 'Or mopping or polishing or scrubbing.'

'Whatever makes you think I taught *dusting*?' asked Miss Burgess, putting the dried dung back in the cupboard. 'That *would* have been boring.'

'I found a timetable.' Phoebe poked it accusingly at Miss Burgess. 'It belonged to a girl called Ruby Dove.'

Miss Burgess took the timetable in her big, freckled fingers. She scrutinized the flimsy piece of paper. '1880!' she boomed. 'Just how old do you think I am?' Then she said, 'Actually, this is quite fascinating.'

Phoebe leaned a bit closer. 'Is it?'

'You've found a timetable from when this place was a servants' school,' Miss Burgess explained. 'That's what it was originally, long before it was a school for mixed infants. Those poor little orphan girls, they were kept hard at it, weren't they? Twelve hours a day of cleaning. That's outrageous! And it wasn't just flicking a feather duster about. Not in those days. It was really hard work. You had to get down on your knees and scrub floors, scour greasy pots –'

Suddenly Miss Burgess seemed more human. Phoebe dared to interrupt her. 'Did you say *orphan* girls?' she asked.

'That's right,' said Miss Burgess, nodding. 'At twelve years old they were sent out here to be trained in cleaning. Then, after a year, they got sent out to posh houses, to be scullery maids or housemaids. And do loads more cleaning. Ruby Dove must have been one of those girls.'

She was only a kid, Phoebe was thinking. She was only about a year older than me.

Instantly she felt sorry for Ruby Dove, although she knew nothing about her except her name – and that she had beautiful handwriting.

'Didn't she ever have any *fun*?' Phoebe hadn't meant to say that out loud, but Miss Burgess answered.

'I don't think you were supposed to have fun at Servants' School,' said Miss Burgess grimly.

She flung the door of her cupboard wide

open. 'Let's see what else we've got in here.'

Oh no, cringed Phoebe. Not the Nature Cupboard again!

'Actually,' added Miss Burgess, 'that name Ruby Dove rings a bell. I think I've got –'

'Look out!' Phoebe cried out a warning. 'Your cupboard's been taken over by spiders!'

As Miss Burgess rescued an armadillo shell and a porcupine prickle, dozens of fat, speckled spiders shot everywhere. Some scuttled all over her hands, even up her arms.

Miss Burgess didn't shriek. She didn't even shake them off in disgust.

'They're more scared of me than I am of them,' she said calmly, picking one out of her orange hair.

Where had Phoebe heard that before? Finn was always saying it. It was supposed to make you feel sorry for spiders. Well, it never worked for me, thought Phoebe, shuddering.

Miss Burgess parted the cobwebs that hung like tattered flags from every shelf. She did it very gently, so as not to break them.

'There's a biscuit tin of very old documents back here somewhere,' she said, rootling about.

She pulled out a rusty tin. 'Now, let me see.' She prised open the lid and sorted through some bits of paper.

'Here it is!' she said triumphantly. 'I knew I'd heard that name before.'

She handed a small piece of grey card to Phoebe. It was a certificate of some sort. But there was no gold lettering on it. Nothing that said, WELL DONE! It was written in purple ink, in small, mean, spiky handwriting.

'*Ruby Dove, First Prize for Polishing*,' it said. And it was signed by Lady Withers.

'Lady Withers lived in The Lair for many years,' explained Miss Burgess, 'with her husband, Lord Withers, a keen arachnologist. His spider collection was world famous! Of course, I'm talking about over a hundred years ago. Lady Withers took a special interest in this school. She chose all her servants from it.'

'Do you think Ruby Dove went to be her servant?' asked Phoebe.

She imagined poor Ruby scrubbing stone floors in that creepy fortress, at six in the morning, when it was still pitch-black and icy cold. Just the thought of it made her shiver.

'I don't know,' said Miss Burgess. 'She

might have done, if she was good at polishing and cleaning. I expect Lady Withers had her eye on her. Did you find out anything else about her?'

'About who?'

'This girl Ruby Dove, of course. You might find something up in your attic. That's where they slept, all the little girls training to be servants. They were probably crammed in there like kippers. By the way, have you got a carrier bag?'

Phoebe found a big yellow carrier bag. Miss Burgess began shovelling her belongings into it.

Then she said, 'I forgot about these. They've been hanging round the place for donkey's years. Look, July 1880, this one's dated. They're monthly magazines, especially for servant girls. You can have them if you like.'

'Can I?' said Phoebe. Despite herself, she was interested. She hadn't been interested in anything much since they'd moved here.

But the magazine's title was enough to put you off. *Arm Oil and Elbow Grease* it was called. And when you opened one up it was even

worse. There were no pictures. Just page after tatty yellow page of tiny print about cleaning: *How To Polish A Silver Teapot, How To Make A Fire Grate Sparkle.*

'They didn't have to *read* these, did they?' said Phoebe. 'They're really boring.'

'That's probably all there *was* to read,' said Miss Burgess. 'I'm guessing they wouldn't have been allowed story books. That might have given them ideas above their station.'

Miss Burgess took a last look into the Nature Cupboard.

'That's it then,' she said, tipping an elephant's toenail into her carrier bag. 'The rest is only fit for the dustbin, I'm afraid.'

Phoebe followed her to the back door. There was a small cobbled yard outside, surrounded by high spiked railings.

'This used to be our playground,' said Miss Burgess. There was a pause and she seemed lost in thought. 'I hope you have some happy times in the Old School,' she told Phoebe. 'I certainly did.'

Were her pale blue eyes even more watery? Hard to tell because, just at that moment, she hid them behind her mirror shades. Then she seemed to make a decision. She dug in her carrier bag and got out Ruby Dove's polishing certificate.

'You might as well keep this,' she said to Phoebe. 'Since you seem to be curious about her,' she added, with some surprise.

She grasped her hiking stick and carrier bag full of memories.

'Goodbye then!' she roared in her foghorn voice. She clumped down the gravel drive and off over the moors.

Phoebe put the little collection of *Arm Oil and Elbow Grease* in her bedroom. She slipped Ruby Dove's timetable and first prize for polishing inside the top magazine on the pile. Then she went outside to take her dad a mug of tea.

Dad was a long way from the house, still wrestling with the rhododendrons. It looked like they'd swallowed him up.

'Blasted plants!' he said to Phoebe. 'They don't want to be cut down.' They were ancient, with twisted, woody stems. 'They've probably been here since this place was built.' He wiped his forehead. 'I don't know who's winning, me or them.'

It was a jungle down there. A place where moorland and garden mingled. There had been a garden wall to keep the wild moorland out, but most of it had fallen down long ago.

Dad took a swig of tea. 'Want to see something?' he asked Phoebe.

Phoebe had been about to make some excuse and dash back to the house. She'd suddenly felt uneasy. The skin at the back of her neck started prickling. She reached up to rub it. She'd felt like this before at the very edge of the garden. As though there was someone here besides herself and Dad. Someone watching from the wilderness.

'Can you smell anything?' she asked Dad, looking round nervously.

There was a strong, nose-tingling whiff of lavender. Phoebe recognized it – Gran used it in her aromatherapy foot spa. But there was no lavender in the garden. Only tough plants like rhododendrons and heather grew up there on the windy fell tops.

Dad said, 'Look what I've found. This must have been their postbox. It was completely overgrown. It hasn't seen daylight for years.'

A chunk of the old garden wall was still

standing. The postbox was set into it. It was dark green, made out of cast iron. There would have been a door on it once. But the door was missing now. You could reach right inside it. There was nothing in there, only a heap of dry, withered leaves blown in by the wind.

'How old is that postbox?' asked Phoebe.

Dad shrugged. 'It was probably put here when the place was first built, like these darn rhododendrons. It was a school for scullery maids or something back then –'

'A Servants' School,' Phoebe corrected him.

Dad looked mildly surprised. 'How did you know that? Anyway, the postman would've walked up here every day to deliver the letters to this box. Any they wanted collecting they would've left in here for him. Save him walking that extra bit up to the school, I suppose. It's nice to find it though, isn't it? It's a part of the history of the Old School. I like things like that.'

But Phoebe was hardly listening. That smell of lavender hadn't gone away . It seemed to be getting more powerful. Phoebe didn't like it. It wasn't a fresh, flowery smell. It was old-

fashioned and stuffy. It caught in your throat.

Dad gulped the last of his tea. 'By the way,' he said, 'did that strange old bird come and collect her stuff?'

'Miss Burgess?' said Phoebe. 'Yes, she did.' Phoebe still hadn't worked out what she thought about Miss Burgess.

I'd hate her for my teacher, she was thinking. She'd already decided that. Talking to you like you were a toddler. Boring you with buffalo dung from her Nature Cupboard.

But, on the plus side, if there was trouble, she'd be a good person to have backing you up. None of the baddies would lay a finger on you. Not if they had to get past her first.

That smell seemed to be following her like a creeping fog.

'Dad! You must be able to smell it now.'

Dad shook his head. 'I've got a stinking cold. I can't smell anything.'

Phoebe had to find fresh air. She left Dad fighting with the rhododendrons. She hadn't gone far when she whirled round.

What was that? Was someone else there? She had just heard a spooky, jangling sound. Like wind chimes hung in trees.

'Don't be stupid!' she scolded herself in teacherish tones Miss Burgess would have been proud of. 'There's nothing there. What are you scared for?'

On the wide gravel drive the smell vanished. She went crunching along it. There were no strange noises behind her. It was only the wind in the rhododendron bushes.

Chapter Three

Next morning, Finn, carrying his zebra spider in a matchbox, set off for The Lair to see his hero, Dr Clinton C. Clinton, the spider psychologist.

'He's just brilliant,' Finn told his spider. 'You'll like him.'

The doctor only had to look at your spider and he could tell you instantly what was wrong with it. It didn't have to be a great beast of a spider, a tarantula or something. It could be tiny, no bigger than a pinhead. And he'd still be able to sort out its problems.

'Your spider's bored. She needs more excitement in her life. More challenges. Let a wasp go in her tank! Your spider is the sensitive, shy type. He doesn't like being looked at. He needs more places to hide.'

Some sad people criticized his methods. They said, 'You can't psychoanalyse spiders! Spiders aren't human. Spiders are just – spiders.'

But Finn knew different. Each of his spiders was an individual. Only an idiot would treat a wolf spider and a funnel-web spider the same. Of all the people he knew, only Dr Clinton C. Clinton gave spiders proper respect.

The closer you got to Dr Clinton's place, the stranger it seemed. The Lair had no walls, no fences. But the rocky ridge it was built on seemed to be some kind of garden. Crevices were stuffed with ferns, heather dripped over craggy ledges.

'Ow!' Finn had stubbed his toe on something. He looked down. It was a head.

It had fallen off a statue. Finn stopped to stare. There were six marble ladies in a circle. They had started out milky white. But now they were blotched with brown, crusty lichen.

This place must have been dead posh once, thought Finn.

They had their arms raised, as if they were dancing. They had once been graceful. But now they just looked grotesque. There were so

many bits of them missing. Over the years, ears had broken off, and noses and heads. Arms had snapped off and lay scattered around.

How freaky, Finn thought, shuddering.

It was the most melancholy garden he'd ever seen. A few green plants peeped out here and there. But mostly it was just rock, as grey and lifeless as the craters of the moon.

What's this then? thought Finn.

Just past the ring of dancing ladies was a little house. It was garden-shed size, but made out of stone. Finn tried the door. It was locked. He peered through the windows. It was gloomy inside. What was in there? He saw pipes looping like snakes, a big iron wheel. Was it some kind of machine?

But his zebra spider was making the matchbox vibrate. She was restless. She seemed as impatient as Finn to meet the great Dr Clinton.

'Let's go,' said Finn.

You had to watch your step here. It wasn't very welcoming. The ground was as full of holes as a coral reef. You could have a nasty fall if you weren't careful.

But these holes seemed to be man-made. Some were tiny – the size of a Smarties tube. Some you could post a dinner plate through. What were they there for?

On impulse, Finn stamped on the rock.

'Ooomm!' A note sounded, like a soft drumbeat. Finn jumped back. Was it hollow under this garden? He knelt down, put his eye to one of the bigger holes. But all he could see was inky blackness.

How weird is that?, Finn marvelled. Stone noses (and other body bits) littered about, machines in little locked houses, holes deliberately drilled through hard rock. It didn't make sense.

But he had other, more urgent things to think about. He was on a mission to find his hero. He climbed on, up to The Lair.

The house was so grand, so intimidating, that Finn almost decided to turn round and head back home. But Dr Clinton's metallic-blue Harley Davidson was parked at the front. That reassured him. However scary the house, a fellow spider freak lived inside.

Feeling bolder, Finn strode up to the front door. It was made of thick, carved oak. There was no doorbell on it, no knocker. You could knock all day until your knuckles got bloody and no one would hear you inside. Finn knocked all the same. No answer.

Maybe he's been called to a spider emergency, thought Finn.

It happened sometimes. The doctor had talked about it on his TV show. Some frantic spider-owner would e-mail him: 'Help! My spider's curled up its legs. It's lost the will to live.' And Dr Clinton would pay you a personal visit and bring your spider back from the brink of death. Or not. He wasn't God – he didn't win all the time. Sometimes, if a spider had just decided to die, there was nothing even he could do.

Finn climbed over more rocks to look in at a window. It was a long, leaded window, with stained glass at the top. In the sunshine, the colours would glow red, green and yellow. But it was a dull day today. No light sparkled off the windows of The Lair. It seemed closed and shut up, a dead house. No signs of life at all. Except that familiar bike parked outside.

Finn looked in. He couldn't see much through those tiny panes. Just a hint of glossy oak furniture, a flash of heavy red velvet curtains. It was all in deep shadow.

I'll have one more try to find him, he decided. Then I'll go home.

None of this felt right somehow. Finn was very confused. On TV, Dr Clinton seemed friendly. He shared your passion for spiders. He was one of the good guys. But his house didn't send out those signals. Strange holes in his rock garden tried to break your ankle. No one answered your knock.

'Be gone!' The Lair seemed to say. 'Private Property,' it warned. 'Keep Off! Or else!'

Finn didn't know what the 'Or else' was. Perhaps fierce black hounds, foaming at the mouth, would rush out and chase you. It felt like that kind of place. He'd been feeling uneasy ever since he'd climbed through that spooky stone garden.

'Finn, you made a big mistake coming here,' he told himself.

He felt suddenly empty. As hollow inside as those rocks sounded. Maybe it was hunger. There was a deep-crust pepperoni pizza in the freezer back home. Perhaps he'd try to see his hero another time.

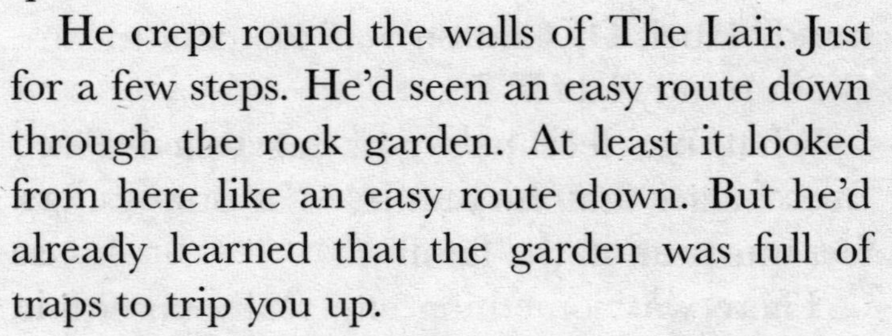

'OK, we're leaving now,' whispered Finn. There was no one to hear him except his zebra spider.

He crept round the walls of The Lair. Just for a few steps. He'd seen an easy route down through the rock garden. At least it looked from here like an easy route down. But he'd already learned that the garden was full of traps to trip you up.

As he tiptoed past another window, a movement inside the house caught his eye.

It's him!

He had a clear view this time. It was the kitchen window. It wasn't split up into dozens of diamond panes.

And Dr Clinton was in there, wearing jeans, T-shirt and a frilly apron. It wasn't the frilly apron that bothered Finn. His dad wore a pinny to wash up. It was what Dr Clinton was wearing on his feet.

Those are really naff open-toed sandals! Finn decided in stern, disapproving tones.

They weren't even trekking sandals – the ones you pay a fortune for in sports shops. No, these were nerdy leather ones, like Finn's granddad wore on the beach. Finn couldn't believe anyone as cool as Dr Clinton would dream of being seen dead in them. On TV he always wore scruffy white trainers, without a trendy label. Dr Clinton was too cool to care about trendy labels.

What big feet he's got! marvelled Finn. Even bigger than his auntie, Miss Burgess. Big feet must run in the family.

There was something else really unsettling about him. His nose looked slippery. It glistened in the gloom, with a greasy, sweaty shine. It didn't look like that on telly. Finn would have noticed.

Maybe the make-up lady slaps powder on it before the programme, thought Finn doubtfully.

But he was even more mixed up now. It felt like someone was playing tricks with his mind. He stared again through the window. What he saw next turned his world upside down.

Dr Clinton was cleaning. He was fussing around, dusting the toaster, polishing the stainless steel kettle, scrubbing at some almost invisible stain on a worktop. Then he picked up a feather duster with a very long handle. Finn watched as if in a dream.

Dr Clinton raised his oily conk to the kitchen ceiling. He'd spotted something.

'No,' whispered Finn, appalled. 'He isn't going do that! Dr Clinton C. Clinton would never do that. Not in a million years!'

But he did. He jabbed with the duster and whisked away a perfect spider's web. One like a completed mathematical puzzle – so lovely and symmetrical it must have taken some poor spider hours to spin it.

But it only took Dr Clinton a second to destroy it. He tore it apart and peeled the sticky strands off his feather duster. Then, with a fanatical gleam in his eye, he went looking for more webs.

There was one over the sink. Dr Clinton couldn't reach it. But he wasn't about to give up. He dragged over a kitchen chair and, quick as a cat, sprang up on it. His awful open-toed sandals seemed the size of dustbin lids. His bare white toes wriggled about like fat maggots. No wonder he didn't go out in public looking like that.

Urggh! thought Finn. His fans would throw up.

But what he was doing with that feather

duster was far, far more sickening than the sandals.

He jabbed once more at a web.

Oh no! thought Finn. The spider's at home.

It was a magnificent house spider. One of the biggest Finn had ever seen – the kind of spider Finn would be proud to have as a pet.

Scared to death, it cowered in a corner. It had nowhere to hide, now its web had gone.

Dr Clinton poked it. It fell.

Phew, thought Finn. It's all right.

Spiders are amazingly indestructible. One spider-expert from Oxford went hot-air ballooning. He was high in the sky, above the clouds. And when he scooped at the air with a net he found spiders in it. They were flying, with silken threads behind them, on wind currents. Thousands of metres above the earth! Spiders had crossed the Atlantic Ocean like that and not come to any harm.

Finn saw the house spider scuttle into the sink. Dr Clinton saw it too. He jumped down off the chair.

He'll rescue it now, thought Finn, who still couldn't accept what he'd just seen. He'll let it go in a dark corner where it's safe.

When his hero handled spiders on TV, it was always very gently. 'They're more scared of you than you are of them.' That was Dr Clinton's second favourite saying.

Dr Clinton peered into the sink. Above his slippery nose, his eyes narrowed. He turned on the hot tap.

Finn opened his mouth to shout, 'NO!' but only a silent scream came out.

The spider clung desperately to the sink edge. It was trying to climb out. Finn could see its four front legs searching for a grip. Too late. Dr Clinton turned the tap full on. He gave the spider a prod. It dropped out of sight. Finn couldn't see it. But he knew what was happening. It would be already dead, curled up like a withered claw. Its body would be swirled closer and closer to the plughole. Then, with a final gurgle, it would be sucked down the drain.

Dr Clinton turned off the tap. He wiped his hands on a tea towel, as if to say, 'Good! That's got rid of that!'

Then he announced in loud, ringing tones, '*The only good spider is a dead spider!*'

Even Finn heard him through the glass. He

almost fainted with shock. His eyes wide with horror, he staggered back from the window. If he hadn't seen it himself he'd never have believed it. If he'd read it in the paper, headline news, *'Spider Psychologist Is Secret Spider Killer,'* he'd have said, 'That's just a big fat lie!'

Finn felt outraged, betrayed, as any faithful fan would. But more than that, he felt this was personal. He had hero-worshipped Dr Clinton C. Clinton for six months, ever since *Pets with Problems* started on TV. And now he'd found out he wasn't a good guy. He was a nasty piece of work.

I wanted to be like him! mourned Finn as he blundered back through the stone garden. Once, when he jumped off a rock and crash-landed near a drill hole, it set off a whole series of strange booming echoes under the ground. But he was too upset to notice.

In his secret fantasies, he'd even imagined that Dr Clinton would take him on as some kind of apprentice, teach him all he knew about spiders. Even let him appear as his assistant on his TV show. And then Finn would be famous too and get lots of letters from girls asking for dates. Well, those dreams were dead and cold as ashes.

What am I going to do now when I grow up? he fretted. His future seemed like a black hole.

And, to make a bad day even worse, when Finn got home he found that, running over the moors, he'd lost the matchbox with his zebra spider inside it. He went straight out again to search. But the moors were so vast and wild and a matchbox so little. He couldn't find her.

He trudged back to the Old School and locked himself away in his bedroom. You could hear his door slam shut all over the house.

Mum was home from work. She knocked on the door.

'Finn? Do you want me to put that pepperoni pizza in the oven for you?'

'No,' growled Finn. 'Go away. I'm not hungry!'

He sat on his bed, with his hands hugging his knees, rocking to and fro. He was thinking about that poor house spider, picturing its terrible panic as it tried to escape from the sink. He was thinking too about his lost zebra spider, imprisoned in a dark matchbox all alone on the moors. Finn couldn't stand it. She'd seemed fairly fed-up lately. That's why he was taking her to see Dr Clinton. Now she would think she had been abandoned.

'It's all your fault, you faker, you cheat, you *pretend* spider enthusiast,' raved Finn.

He had thought Dr Clinton was different. But he was just like 99.9 per cent of the population – prejudiced against spiders.

It's all right if you're little and furry, thought Finn. Everybody goes '*Awwwww!*' They think you're cute and cuddly. They want to protect you! But if you're little and furry with eight legs, that's different. They want to flush you down the loo. Or pulverize you till you're paste! *WHY?* Finn appealed to himself hopelessly. *WHY?* For him it was one of the great mysteries of life.

But it was losing faith in Dr Clinton that caused Finn most distress. He wouldn't have minded finding out that his hero was only human. Everyone's allowed some cheesy clothing. Even Finn himself had a stripy tank top knitted by his gran. Finn could *even* have forgiven Dr Clinton for being a fussy duster.

And perhaps, *accidentally*, wrecking a spider's home. But to see with his own eyes that his idol was an inhuman monster, a cold-blooded murderer of innocent arachnids? It was more than Finn's poor, boiling brain could cope with.

He's sick! decided Finn. He shouldn't be allowed near a spider! I'm never, ever going to watch his show again. I'm going to tell all my friends not to watch it. And I'm going to resign from his fan club!

He took the photo of Dr Clinton C. Clinton from his bedside table and glared ferociously at it. Now he didn't see that smile as warm and friendly. He saw it as smarmy and deceitful. The smile of a secret spider hater.

The photo was signed. Dr Clinton had written '*Spiders Need Friends Too*' under his signature.

'You hypocrite!' hissed Finn.

He ripped his ex-hero's photo into a hundred tiny pieces.

Chapter Four

Like Finn, Phoebe was in her bedroom. She opened *Arm Oil and Elbow Grease* – the one where she'd hidden Ruby Dove's first prize for polishing and her timetable. She wanted to have another look at them. How could handwriting be so different? Ruby's was round and flowing. Lady Withers' was prickly, purple and cramped.

Phoebe's eyes wandered to the magazine.

Tips on how to dust a drawing room, it said. *Always dampen your duster. Be sure to dust the ceiling – one spider's web is the sign of a slothful servant.*

Phoebe yawned. Boring! She felt sorry for those poor girls at the Servants' School, having nothing to read but this stuff.

She flicked to the last page. It was headed *Answers to Correspondents.*

What's this? Phoebe wondered. It took her a few seconds to work it out. It seemed to be some sort of problem page, where servant girls' letters were answered. Only it wasn't like modern problem pages, where you can see the readers' letters. Back in 1880 they didn't bother putting them in. They only printed the agony aunt's advice. Phoebe read some of her replies.

To Aggie, scullery maid.

Wear flannel knickerbockers at all times! Grease your nose with best butter if you have a cold! Your handwriting is quite deplorable.

The Servants' Friend

Another reply from The Servants' Friend was even more snooty and mean.

To Millie Slack, parlour maid, read Phoebe.

We decline to answer absurd questions about boys from silly, lovesick servant girls. Attend to your dusting duties! That is our advice! Your handwriting is quite the worst we have ever seen!

The Servants' Friend

What kind of useless advice is that? thought Phoebe angrily. What an old bossy-boots! Why does she go on and on about handwriting? And why does she say 'we' instead of 'I'? She must think she's the queen!

The Servants' Friend's third reply was to Ruby Dove.

'Ruby! I don't believe it,' said Phoebe out loud. 'You didn't write to that snappy old witch, did you? What did you do that for?'

But there was Ruby's reply, in black and white, in the magazine.

To Ruby Dove, student servant.

We are consigning your letter to the waste-paper bin. We refuse to answer your questions until you improve your handwriting. Write again and try harder.

The Servants' Friend

'That's just cruel!' cried Phoebe. Why wouldn't she answer Ruby's questions? 'And what's wrong with Ruby's handwriting anyway?' Phoebe muttered. 'It's a million times better than mine.'

Ruby must have been desperate, thought Phoebe, to write to this awful Victorian agony aunt. But anyone would get desperate, stuck out here on bleak moorland, having to do three hours of dusting before breakfast.

It was tormenting not to be able to see Ruby's letter. What had she written to The Servants' Friend about? What had her problems been? Phoebe really wanted to know.

Then Phoebe had a brilliant idea. Perhaps Ruby *had* tried harder, *had* written another letter, like The Servants' Friend told her to? She looked at the dates on the magazines. This one was May 1880. She searched through the others. June was missing. But here was July 1880. Feverishly she found the *Answers to Correspondents* page, ran her finger down the list of replies.

Put mustard powder on your chilblains! . . . Grease your nose with best butter! . . . Slouching is a very bad habit! . . . Do what you are told! . . . Attend to your duties! . . . Your scrubbing brush needs harder bristles! . . . Be more obedient! . . . IMPROVE YOUR HANDWRITING! . . .

Phoebe's finger stopped at '*To Ruby Dove*'.

She *did* try again! thought Phoebe triumphantly. And this time The Servants' Friend had given Ruby some advice.

Your handwriting is hardly improved! Nevertheless, we will be kind and answer your questions. You say you do not wish to be a housemaid. That you have dreams. Servants should not have dreams. Pray forget such vain and foolish fancies. They are pure self-indulgence! Try to be more humble. Repeat to yourself every day, 'IT IS MY DESTINY TO DUST' and strive to be grateful.

The Servants' Friend

It was the last straw. Phoebe sprang off her bed. She was boiling with rage. She forgot all this had happened over a hundred years ago. She shouted out loud as if Ruby Dove could hear her. 'Don't listen to her, Ruby! She doesn't know what she's talking about. Her advice is a load of old rubbish!'

Wild and fantastic ideas were whizzing about in Phoebe's brain. If only I could have answered Ruby's letters instead of her, she was thinking. Crushing someone's dreams like that was criminal. And in such a sneery, ruthless way. It shouldn't be allowed! thought Phoebe.

Why shouldn't Ruby Dove do what she wants? If I was her friend, I'd say, 'Go for it!'

Hardly knowing what she was doing, Phoebe found a pen in her hand. She tore a page out of the back of her diary and scribbled her own letter. Her outrage was so powerful and strong that her hand was shaking as she wrote.

Dear Ruby Dove,

Don't listen to that Servants' Friend, she's rubbish. Listen to ME instead. Everyone's allowed to have dreams. You don't have to be a servant all your life. DUSTING IS DEAD BORING!

Love, Phoebe

She'd thought the letter would relieve her feelings. But it didn't.

What's the use? she thought suddenly. She couldn't get through to Ruby. All this had happened in the past.

'Forget it,' Phoebe told herself.

But she was so mad at The Servants' Friend, so sorry for Ruby Dove that she couldn't.

Phoebe had to get some air. She felt her

brain was about to burst. She knew that a great injustice had been done. She wanted to put it right somehow. But it was all too long ago. She went storming round the garden, muttering angrily to herself. 'Wicked old witch!' She couldn't bear being so helpless.

Then she was closed in by dark rhododendrons. How had she got here? She still had the letter to Ruby Dove scrunched up in her hand.

'Phoebe, is that you?'

Phoebe whirled round, her heart racing.

'Phoebe?'

It was only Dad, calling from somewhere in the rhododendrons.

She had no pockets in her clothes. She felt stupid, standing there clasping a letter to a girl who'd lived over a hundred years ago.

Her head was clearing a little. That red rage was fading. Embarrassed, she looked round for a hiding place. She stuck her letter into a rhododendron bush. But it stood out like a white flag. Anyone with half a brain would spot it. She took it out again. Then, before Dad turned up, she stuffed it quickly inside the old postbox, under the dried leaves. She didn't want to explain it to Dad. He'd think she was going crazy.

'I'm giving up,' said Dad as he appeared through the bushes. 'I'm going for some lunch.' He looked at Phoebe more closely. 'You all right?' he asked her. 'You look a bit upset.'

Phoebe shrugged. 'I'm all right,' she said.

They walked together to the Old School.

'Are you sure you can't smell anything?' Phoebe asked Dad. She'd just got another powerful whiff of lavender. This time it made her feel dizzy. She put a hand on a tree trunk to steady herself. Gran's foot spa had never affected her like this. This was like an attack on her brain.

'I told you,' said Dad. 'I've got a cold. I couldn't even smell Finn's socks. Not if he waved them right under my nose.'

'You should grease your nose with best butter,' advised Phoebe sternly. 'And wear flannel knickerbockers to keep warm.' She wagged a fussy finger at Dad. 'Are you wearing them today?'

'Er, no,' admitted Dad, sounding bewildered. 'I've got boxers on. That best

butter thing – is that the latest cold cure or something? I've just been taking aspirins.'

They were out on the gravel drive now. The air here was fresh and clean, not lavender-tainted.

Phoebe gave her head a savage shake. It seemed to do some good – she felt back in control. Did she really just say what she thought she'd said? She must have done because Dad was asking, 'That's a bit of a waste of butter, isn't it?'

'Someone said it was good for colds,' mumbled Phoebe, flustered. 'I read it in a magazine.'

'Well, they're talking out the top of their head. Someone should write and tell them.'

I wish I could, thought Phoebe. I really, really wish I could. Then she had a different wish.

I wish I knew what Ruby Dove's dream was. Did she want to be a fine lady? Ride in a carriage? Be waited on hand, foot and finger and not have to do any more cleaning?

'I'm going up to the attic,' Phoebe told Dad.

'What for?'

'Oh,' answered Phoebe vaguely, 'just looking for something.'

For ages, she didn't find anything interesting. Most of the junk was from when this place was an infant school. Broken bits of chalk, bent plastic hoops and tatty reading books.

Once, taking a rest from searching, she stared out the attic windows. It was dusk. The moors were grey and gloomy. But Finn was still out there with a torch. He kept shining it into the heather. He seemed to be looking for something too.

She switched on the dim light. The attic looked like a cave now, with deep corners of dark shadows.

Fed up, Phoebe tipped out another dusty cardboard box. Just loads of papers. Then she found something. It was a scruffy, leather-bound notebook. At first, Phoebe hardly noticed the book. It didn't seem important, compared to what fell out of its pages. She picked up the old photograph. It wasn't all there. It seemed to have been torn in two. But on the bit that was left was a picture of Ruby Dove.

Her name was on the back of it in handwriting Phoebe didn't recognize. It wasn't

Lady Withers' or Ruby's either. It said, '12 November, 1880, Ruby Dove receiving first prize for polishing –.' Whatever else it had said was gone with the missing half.

The photo was grey and cracked and faded, but Phoebe felt she'd found golden treasure. Here was Ruby herself in her Servants' School uniform. It was really frumpy. A shapeless black frock and thick, black, woolly stockings and clumpy boots.

Oh Ruby, thought Phoebe, shaking her head. They never made you wear that, did they?

Ruby was holding up her certificate for the camera. She wasn't smiling. She had a serious, worried face.

I expected her to look different, thought Phoebe. What had she expected? Someone delicate and dreamy, too weedy-looking for the heavy work that Victorian servant girls had to do? But Ruby Dove's photo showed a big tough girl. She looked like she could lug two buckets of coal up three flights of stairs, no problem.

Phoebe stared straight into Ruby Dove's eyes. 'What were your dreams, Ruby, that you wrote about in your letter to that mean old agony aunt?'

But Ruby stared back and couldn't answer.

It was only when she was back in her bedroom that Phoebe thought to open the leather-bound book. She couldn't make head or tail of it. What a strange jumble! There were bits of music and mathematical calculations and plans of strange machines and maps of what looked like underground caves. She almost threw it aside.

What a load of old rubbish.

Then, as she turned over another page, she felt a thrill of recognition. Those jottings in the margin – she knew that handwriting. They had been written by Ruby Dove.

Finn burst into her bedroom.

'Hey!' said Phoebe, startled. 'Get out! Boys aren't allowed in here!'

'I'd let girls into my bedroom,' protested Finn.

'Yeah, but they wouldn't want to come into your bedroom, would they? They'd probably catch some horrible disease.'

Finn was famously messy. He kept his spiders in perfect order. But apart from that he was a slob. His bedroom was a rat's nest of dirty clothes, empty micro-chip packets and mugs growing furry green mould.

'You seen my zebra spider?' demanded Finn.

It was his last hope. He thought she might have somehow found her way back, like a homing pigeon. 'Never underestimate the talents of spiders,' that's what Dr Clinton always said. Finn wished he hadn't remembered that. He didn't care any more what Dr Clinton said. As far as Finn was concerned, he was a fallen angel.

'He belongs in *Hell*!' muttered Finn grimly.

'Who does?' Phoebe gave him a blank stare.

'I've lost my spider!' wailed Finn.

Phoebe almost replied with a rude, 'So what?' But Finn looked wild-eyed and desperate. Phoebe knew how much he cared about his spiders. He talked about them as if they were people.

'It'd better not have escaped in here,' was all she said.

Finn wasn't looking for a fight either. The day's events had left him badly shaken. His faith in grown-ups, especially grown-ups who

claimed they were fellow spider freaks, was shattered.

He slumped on to Phoebe's bed. She didn't order him off. She, too, had had a strange, unsettling day.

'I looked everywhere for her,' moaned Finn. 'Out on the moors. In dark den-type places where spiders go. I even looked in that old postbox thing at the end of the drive.'

'When did you look in there?' demanded Phoebe.

Maybe he'd searched it before she hid Ruby's letter. She felt pretty stupid for writing it now. She didn't know what had come over her.

'I looked just now. I shone my torch in there. Have you been down that end of the garden? There's this stuffy smell, *phew*, like old lady's scent. And I heard this jangly noise – What's all that about?'

Phoebe felt her stomach clench, tight as a fist. 'Come on,' she threatened, 'give me the letter.'

'I don't know what you're talking about.'

'You know! The letter you found in the postbox.'

'I haven't got a letter. Honest! The postbox was empty – except for some woodlice under the leaves. Did you know another name for woodlice is pill bugs? Because in olden times people used to take them as medicine. I suppose when they roll up tight they do look like little pills – if you're a bit thick, that is. Anyway, they used to swallow them alive. That's really cruel! I hope they tickled on the way down.'

'Don't try to change the subject!' Phoebe interrupted him in her most dangerous voice. 'You're lying about that letter. I always know when you're lying.'

'OK, OK,' said Finn, suddenly surrendering. 'I don't want your stupid letter anyway.'

He fumbled in his pocket, threw the letter on to the bed and stomped out of the room.

For a long time Phoebe didn't pick the letter up. She just stared at it.

A strange, electric tingling was creeping up her spine.

It was a letter all right. But not her scribbled, crumpled note. It was sealed up in a long, creamy envelope. And on the front it said, *To Phoebe.*

She'd got a reply.

Her very first thought was that Finn had read what she'd written to Ruby Dove. That he was messing about, playing some kind of trick.

But when she tore it open she knew straightaway that Finn wasn't involved. It wasn't his style. Finn's jokes weren't this clever. He thought making rude, raspberry noises was funny.

Phoebe's hands were shaking as she unfolded the letter. It was a very short reply.

We refuse to engage in any correspondence with you until you improve your deplorable handwriting.

The Servants' Friend

The interfering old witch! were Phoebe's first thoughts. That letter wasn't addressed to her. How dare she read it! I wrote it for Ruby. What's she doing sticking her nose in? Hasn't she caused enough trouble?

It was only with her next thoughts that she let her mind admit the full horror of what was happening.

She dropped the letter as if it had suddenly

burst into flames. She felt hot and sick.

She'd just been written to by someone who was alive in 1880. Either The Servants' Friend had found the secret of everlasting life, or Phoebe was getting letters from a ghost.

Chapter Five

'What are you doing?' Finn asked Phoebe when he came down for breakfast the next morning.

'Practising my handwriting,' said Phoebe.

'Eh?' said Finn. He thought he'd gone deaf. He raked out his ears. 'Did you say, *practising your handwriting?'*

'Yes,' said Phoebe, as if it was something kids did for fun all the time. She had a big bottle of ink and Dad's posh fountain pen. All around her were screwed-up pieces of paper, covered with words and letters.

Finn frowned. 'Why don't you just use the computer instead of messing about like that, with ink and stuff?'

'I can't,' said Phoebe. 'I'm writing this letter to someone who's got handwriting on the brain. Handwriting and cleaning, actually.'

Finn looked shocked. Could such a person really exist? He could believe more easily in an eight-tentacled purple alien from the planet Zarg.

'Anyway,' said Phoebe, 'I've got to do this handwriting really well, or she won't answer my letter.'

There were butterflies in her stomach, as if she was taking an important test in school. At this moment, she was more worried about her handwriting, than the fact that, yesterday, she'd somehow made contact with a dead person – and was trying to do it again.

Finn jigged about uneasily. He ached to tell someone about Dr Clinton. C. Clinton. He longed to share his shock and horror at what he'd seen yesterday, through the window of The Lair.

Over and over in his head, he saw that poor, doomed spider scrabbling to escape and Dr Clinton's own hand turning on the hot tap. He tried to find explanations, excuses. But what excuses could there be? Except that Dr Clinton was a sham – a caring spider psychologist in public, but in private, a cold-hearted killer.

Finn might have asked Phoebe for help, but she was in a funny mood this morning. She looked pale and tired, as if she hadn't slept last night either. She seemed far away, out of reach – as if she had troubles of her own to deal with. And Dad had problems too. He was down in the cellar worrying about plumbing.

'You know,' he'd told Finn last night, 'I don't actually know *where* our water comes from. There must be underground springs round here somewhere.'

'You going out?' Phoebe asked Finn, looking up from her letter.

'Yep. I'm looking for my spider again.'

'Will you post this letter for me?'

'Where?' asked Finn, baffled. The nearest post office was down in the village, five miles away.

'In that old postbox in the garden, where you looked for your spider.'

Finn laughed out loud in astonishment.

'No one uses that any more. You can't post letters in that!'

'Just do it!' said Phoebe. She didn't want to go down there herself. It was too spooky. And she'd had all the spookiness she could stand.

Last night she'd checked under her bed and in her wardrobe. She'd slept with the light on. Getting letters from ghosts makes you very jumpy.

Phoebe folded up the letter she'd written. She was proud of it. It was business-like and got straight to the point. It said, in her very best handwriting:

Dear Servants' Friend,

Stop sticking your big nose into Ruby Dove's life. I mean it. And stop giving her such rubbish advice. I'm her friend now, her real friend. She doesn't need you. So tell me you'll stop. Will you stop? Tick box

Yes ☐

No ☐

I'll think about it ☐

Phoebe

It seemed madness to write a reply. It was like encouraging ghosts. But she couldn't help herself. She was on a mission – to save Ruby Dove from an evil agony aunt. Somehow, the postbox had put her in touch with The Servants' Friend. It was too good a chance to waste. She mustn't let fear stop her.

Maybe she, Phoebe, could make a difference. Maybe, just maybe, she could change history.

She'd got an envelope from Mum. She wrote *The Servants' Friend* on the outside and was just about to slide her letter in when she had another thought.

PS, she added to the letter, *I know who you are.*

Let's see what the old bat says to that! thought Phoebe.

It hadn't been too hard. The handwriting gave it away. Phoebe, after she'd got over her first shock, had compared the letter Finn had brought her with Ruby Dove's first prize for polishing. It hit you right in the eye. That mean, spiky, purple handwriting matched up exactly. Lady Withers and The Servants' Friend were one and the same person.

'You know that big house called The Lair?' Phoebe asked Finn as she handed him the envelope. 'Who lives there now?'

'I don't want to talk about it!' said Finn abruptly, and he dashed out of the kitchen.

Phoebe stared after him. What's up with him? she thought.

But she had too many other questions to

worry her. Would she get a reply this time? How long would it take? A few hours or a few days? Could she reach Ruby Dove through the postbox? She'd thought of writing Ruby another letter, but she was sure that The Servants' Friend would get to it first.

It would be just like her, thought Phoebe. I don't want that nosy old witch knowing what I write to Ruby. No, writing to Ruby would have to wait. First, thought Phoebe. I've got to get rid of Lady Withers.

She was surprised at how fearless she felt. Her anger made her strong. And determined. 'It's just pathetic!' she muttered fiercely. 'Telling a poor servant girl she can't have dreams when you're a rich Lady who lives in a castle!'

Finn almost didn't post Phoebe's letter. He was so anxious to get to the moors to look for his spider that he nearly forgot. It was only at the last moment that he swerved off into the rhododendrons.

Without even thinking about it, he shoved the letter into the postbox , under the leaves.

He wasn't curious about it. He had too many other things on his mind.

Spiders could go for a long time without food. But, sooner or later, his pet would get hungry. Then what would she do, shut up in a matchbox?

If she dies, thought Finn mournfully, it'll be that Dr Clinton C. Clinton's fault. I wouldn't have lost her if it hadn't been for him.

In his present mood, Finn was ready to blame Dr Clinton for anything: global warming; the fact that his breakfast Crispy Wheaty Pops had gone soggy in the milk . . .

The lavender smell sneaked up on him before he noticed it. It had wrapped itself round his neck like a tight, woolly scarf. It was throttling him. He opened his mouth to gasp for fresh air, but instead he sucked in more scent. It filled his mouth, his lungs, invaded his brain . . .

Worries about his spider were whisked from Finn's mind. He thought for a split second, Hey! What's happening to me? Then he didn't think anything except, That postbox is a bit dusty.

He ran his finger along the top and clucked in a disapproving way. '*Tsk, tsk!* I must bring my cleaning things down here right *now*!'

Chapter Six

At lunchtime, Phoebe found Finn in his bedroom. She wanted to ask him whether he'd posted her letter. She also wanted to keep him sweet, so that he'd go down to see if there was any reply. She asked him, 'Did you find your zebra spider?'

Finn frowned at her. 'What are you talking about?' He had a yellow duster in his hand.

Phoebe frowned back. 'What's wrong with your nose?' She reached out to touch it, then yanked her hand back. 'Ugh, it's all slimy. What's that dripping off it? No, don't tell me!'

'It's best butter, of course,' said Finn smugly. 'I've got a cold coming. You haven't seen any flannel knickerbockers knocking about, have you?'

Little warning bells were ringing at the back of Phoebe's mind.

Finn dabbed fussily at his bedside table.

'What are you doing?' asked Phoebe.

'I'm tidying up,' said Finn.

Phoebe's mouth fell open in an astonished 'O'.

'But you never tidy up!' she told Finn. 'When Mum tidies up in here she fills three bin bags. She says she should hire a skip.'

Finn looked hurt. 'Cleanliness is very important,' he announced primly. 'Cleanliness is next to Godliness.'

He flicked the duster over his collection of Judge Dredd comics. He folded up his boxers. He paired up his socks, rolled each pair into a tight little sausage and packed them neatly away in his drawer.

'Why are you talking like this?' begged Phoebe, distressed and bewildered. 'You sound like *HER*. Have you been reading *Arm Oil and Elbow Grease*?'

'I haven't got time for reading,' said Finn. 'Reading wastes precious cleaning time. Why aren't you busy cleaning? The devil makes work for idle hands, you know.'

He pushed Phoebe roughly aside. 'Excuse me,' he said. 'I've got things to do. I must dampen my duster and re-grease my nose.'

Phoebe heard him clattering down the stairs. What was he was chanting? '*My destiny is to dust. My destiny is to dust –*'

What's wrong with him? she wondered. Dark suspicions were already crowding into her mind, but she pushed them aside. She had a more urgent worry.

You'll have to go down to that postbox yourself, she thought, taking a deep breath.

As she passed the kitchen, Finn was searching in the fridge for some butter. 'No, no,' she heard him tutting. 'Lo-fat spread just *will not* do.'

Phoebe plunged into the rhododendrons. Their tough, twisty stems tried to trip her up, spike holes in her T-shirt. She tore away from them and ended up panting, by the old postbox. She was trembling with fear and a queer excitement. Had The Servants' Friend written back?

There was a letter. A creamy, marbled envelope that smelt, very faintly, of lavender. Phoebe saw her name on the front in that familiar, cramped purple handwriting. She ripped it open with shaking hands.

Your grammar is deplorable. Your use of abbreviations is vulgar. The tone of your letter is most immodest. We cannot answer your question until you write to us in a more polite manner. Your handwriting is still very bad. We are bound to tell the truth.

The Servants' Friend

'No!' Phoebe screamed out with rage and frustration. She forgot about being scared. She crumpled the letter in her fist.

'*I asked you about Ruby!*' she yelled furiously. 'I want you to mind your own business. Stop telling her she can't have dreams. Dreams – *that's* what's important. Handwriting doesn't matter! Why do you keep going on and on about things that don't matter?'

And there was another question to ask that sneaky old bat.

'What have you done to my brother, Finn? He's been acting funny ever since he came down to post my letter. Have you brain-washed him? Like you tried to brainwash me? He's turning into a tidiness freak!'

There were no answers, of course, from Lady Withers. Phoebe didn't expect them. You could only reach her by letter. And then only if your handwriting was up to scratch. But something was happening in that wild part of the garden. The air around Phoebe felt chilly. She was shivering, as if she was trapped in a giant freezer.

There was a sudden, harsh jangling.

Phoebe jumped. Who's there?

The jangling came again. Louder and more threatening. Then suddenly Phoebe felt the presence of such cold malevolence, such icy anger, that she bolted in panic.

'It's The Servants' Friend!' Phoebe's brain was shrieking. 'It's *her*!'

There was the lavender smell, creeping along the ground like marsh gas. Phoebe outran it, smashing through the rhododendrons. She didn't want to end up brainwashed, like Finn, greasing her nose with best butter and turning up on the first day of her new school wearing flannel knickerbockers.

When she felt safe, in the Old School playground, Phoebe collapsed against the iron spikes. Her legs wouldn't carry her any further. She knew she'd got a kind of answer from The Servants' Friend. More of a warning than an answer. The warning was, 'Don't mess with me, you puny, twenty-first century child. I'll crush you like a cockroach if you get in my way.'

It wasn't how Lady Withers would have written it. But it was what she meant. There was no way she would give up her influence over Ruby Dove. Not without a fight. And now it seemed she'd got Finn under her control.

Finn came out of the back door with his nose freshly greased. He had a smug expression on his face and a spray can of Mr Gleam in his hand. He started to polish the dustbins.

'For heaven's sake!' said Phoebe. She didn't like this new Finn. He was like a stranger. The old Finn was permanently puzzled about life. Except, of course, when he was with his spiders. This Finn looked as if he knew all the answers.

'We must not slouch,' he lectured Phoebe in a priggish voice. 'It's a very bad habit. We must practise walking around with books on our heads.'

'Get lost!' snapped Phoebe. 'Go and do some dusting indoors.'

She sounded forceful and confident, but she didn't feel like that.

What have I got myself into? she was thinking. She'd taken on an enemy more scary and powerful then she'd ever imagined. But still, she wasn't going to give up. The battle for Ruby Dove had just begun.

'Except I think I need some help,' whispered Phoebe. She suddenly felt very weedy and vulnerable. She needed someone tough. Someone who didn't think it was their destiny to dust. Who had the strength of mind to say 'What rot!' to all Lady Withers' advice.

And, just at that moment, Miss Burgess came striding over the moors. Her collapsible titanium hiking stick and teacup glittered, like a Jedi knight's sword.

'Miss Burgess!' shouted Phoebe frantically, like a drowning person who's seen someone to cling to. 'Have you got a minute?'

Chapter Seven

'Well, well,' Miss Burgess boomed, inspecting the bit of photo with Ruby's picture on it. 'This girl would have been a real catch for anyone on the lookout for a good house maid.'

Miss Burgess and Phoebe were in the Old School kitchen. Phoebe was showing Miss Burgess some of her discoveries: the photo, the two replies to Ruby in *Arm Oil and Elbow Grease*.

She'd kept quiet so far about the ghostly replies in the postbox and the fact that Lady Withers and The Servants' Friend were one and the same person. She wasn't sure yet whether to break this news. She wondered now why she'd chosen Miss Burgess to confide in. She was a matter-of-fact, no-

nonsense person. She wouldn't be scared of things that go bump in the night, but she probably wouldn't believe in them either.

'Why?' asked Phoebe. 'Why would they specially want Ruby?'

Miss Burgess looked again at the photo. 'Because she's strong as an ox, that's why. Look at those muscles. She could scrub floors until they gleamed. Put a shine on the copper pans –'

'But Ruby didn't want to do that!' interrupted Phoebe angrily. 'Ruby had other plans! It's just that awful old Servants' Friend who told her it wasn't allowed.'

And now she knew why. Everything fell into place. The last thing Lady Withers wanted was Ruby escaping from the Servants' School. She didn't want Ruby to follow her dream. She wanted her to spend her whole life at The Lair, dusting and cleaning until she dropped dead from overwork.

Phoebe's anger on Ruby's behalf blazed up more fiercely than ever. She forgot the power of Lady Withers' evil presence among those dark rhododendrons. She felt brave all over again. Ready to go ten rounds with her in a boxing ring.

You awful selfish old witch, she was thinking. You ruined Ruby's entire life, didn't you? Just so you could have some shiny pans!

'So what did Ruby do?' Phoebe begged Miss Burgess. 'Did she follow her dreams? Or did she believe what The Servants' Friend told her – that it was her destiny to dust?'

'We'll probably never find out,' said Miss Burgess, shaking her head. She studied Ruby's photo again. 'Shame it got torn,' she said vaguely, turning it over.

There was a strange, misty expression in her pale blue eyes. Where had that come from? Phoebe had never seen it before.

'I sympathize a great deal with that poor girl,' said Miss Burgess suddenly. 'When I was her age people couldn't see past my muscles. And I had a dream, just like her.'

Phoebe looked at Miss Burgess with new interest.

'Yes,' continued Miss Burgess. 'I was brought up on these wild moors. I wasn't a stick insect, like these modern girls. I had some meat on my bones! Farmers would call on me when their sheep got stuck in ditches. I could wrestle them out single-handed.'

Phoebe looked at Miss Burgess's sturdy legs in their red hiking socks. She could believe that. Miss Burgess probably had pecs like Popeye.

'My parents thought my future was secure,' said Miss Burgess. 'They thought I would stay on the moors for ever, as a sort of roving sheep-rescuer. But, like Ruby Dove, I had my own dreams.'

'What were they?' asked Phoebe. She really wanted to know.

'I wanted to be a teacher,' said Miss Burgess.

'Oh,' said Phoebe, disappointed.

'Well,' said Miss Burgess briskly, the misty look clearing from her eyes, 'it's preferable to sheep wrestling. Most of the time anyway. But the point is,' stressed Miss Burgess, 'that my parents finally relented and I achieved my dream. I wonder what Ruby Dove wanted so badly?'

Phoebe wanted to know that too. She wanted to know, more than anything.

'Did you find anything else in your attic?'

'Only this,' said Phoebe, holding out the battered leather-bound notebook. 'I don't know who it belongs to. But that's Ruby's handwriting in the margins.'

Miss Burgess settled down at the kitchen table. She inspected each page – the music, the maps, the plans of machines – with maddening slowness. What was going on in her head? Hard to tell. Sometimes she turned back to check what she'd read again. Phoebe was jigging about with impatience.

'What's so interesting?' she asked.

'My, my, our tongues are busy as bees today, aren't they?' said Miss Burgess without looking up, as if she was still in charge of a class. Then, in case Phoebe hadn't got the message, she hissed, '*Shhhhh!*'

She wouldn't last two minutes now as a teacher, thought Phoebe scornfully, talking to kids like that. But, all the same, she kept her mouth shut until Miss Burgess had finished.

Finally, Miss Burgess looked up triumphantly from the last page. She was about to roar, 'I think I've discovered Ruby

Dove's dream!' when a slippery nose poked round the kitchen door.

'Anything need cleaning in here?' asked its owner. And Finn shuffled in, like a flat-footed robot, with a pile of spider books from his bedroom balanced on his head. The title of one of the books was *Pooter Hunting for Boys* by Lord Withers.

'What *do* you think you look like?' sighed Phoebe.

'I'm trying to improve my posture,' snapped Finn in his prudish voice. 'Slouching is sinful.'

Finn looked very purposeful. His eyes shone with enthusiasm – for scrubbing and mopping and dusting. He'd been badly infected with the cleaning bug. He was totally neglecting his spiders. The Servants' Friend had really messed up his mind.

'Polish every pot and pan, Make that kitchen spick and span,' droned Finn, as he toddled round, stiff as a peg, wiping the work surfaces.

'Is that tune from the top ten?' enquired Miss Burgess. Sometimes she made an effort to communicate with modern youth. But she didn't try often. She wasn't *that* bothered.

Finn ignored her. He squinted down at the grill pan, which is hard when you can't bend your neck. '*Tut, tut,* look at the state of that,' he fussed. 'That needs a good scrubbing.'

Phoebe sighed. 'That's my brother,' she told Miss Burgess in an expressionless voice, as if everyone's brother spent their summer holidays doing housework with books on their heads while singing dreary little songs about dusting.

'I know!' cried Miss Burgess, in a voice loud enough to make the crockery tinkle. 'We've already met. We share a common interest in pooters. But I must say, he seems very different. He was a dreamy sort of boy when I met him – with a *vivid imagination*,' Miss Burgess added, as if that was a big disadvantage. 'The kind of boy who can't pay attention and stares out the window in class. What's happened to him?'

'Lady Withers happened to him,' said Phoebe flatly. Then she had to spill the beans. It was easy once she'd started. In fact, she'd been aching to do it. Now Finn had been nobbled by Lady Withers, she felt terribly alone. The burden of those spooky letters was more than she could bear.

Miss Burgess listened in the gravest silence. She examined the letters that Phoebe showed her as carefully as she'd inspected the notebook. She compared their spiky purple handwriting with Ruby's polishing certificate.

'There's no doubt,' she said, when Phoebe had finished her story, 'that Lady Withers and The Servants' Friend are one and the same person, but as to the rest of it – there's probably a perfectly logical explanation –'

Oh no! thought Phoebe frantically. She doesn't believe me. I knew she wouldn't! She's going to tell me off. She's going to say, 'You shouldn't have such a *vivid imagination*!'

'On the other hand,' Miss Burgess hesitated, as if she was half-shocked at what she was about to say, 'I've studied some local history. That Lady Withers was a notorious know-all. She loved telling people what to do, especially poor people. Perhaps her spirit does live on. People like her just can't stop interfering. Even being dead doesn't put them off.'

'So you believe me?' said Phoebe. She was so relieved that she couldn't stop shaking.

'Let's say,' Miss Burgess replied cautiously, 'that after thirty years in the teaching profession, nothing surprises me any more.'

'I just wanted her to leave Ruby alone,' wailed Phoebe in despair. 'But now she's got Finn as well.'

With a decisive flick of her wrist Miss Burgess extended her titanium hiking stick and tea cup. 'We'll see about that,' she said.

'Give me that duster *at once*!' she ordered Finn in her sternest, most teacherish tones. Finn clutched his duster like a comfort blanket. It looked as if wild horses couldn't drag it from him.

'AT ONCE!' thundered Miss Burgess.

Startled, Finn handed it over.

Miss Burgess tied the duster on top of the hiking stick and handed it back to Finn. He snatched it eagerly.

'There you are,' she said. 'There's a present for you. It's an extendable cobweb cleaner.'

'An extendable cobweb cleaner!' cried Finn, cuddling his new gift. His eyes shone with happiness. 'It's every lad's dream! It's just what I've always wanted!'

Phoebe shook her head hopelessly. Lady Withers' grip on Finn seemed unbreakable. What if he'd got hold of a pair of flannel knickerbockers? What if he was wearing them right now, under his baggy pants? Phoebe didn't want to think about that. It was too upsetting.

'Go on then,' Miss Burgess urged Finn. 'Try it out. There's a cobweb in that corner.'

Finn's well-buttered conk quivered with delight at the prospect of more cleaning. Even improving his posture wasn't as exciting as this! The books fell off his head, forgotten. Lord Withers' *Pooter Hunting for Boys* slid down his greasy snout as if it was a ski slope.

'I see it,' he cried. 'How did I miss that? It'll have to come down!' Then, 'Silly me,' he scolded himself. 'I haven't dampened my duster!'

He sprang over to the sink, ran the tap. 'You can't do a good dusting job without a damp duster,' he informed Phoebe. 'And another amazing fact about dusting –'

Phoebe groaned. She could feel her eyes glazing over. She wondered if people really could die of boredom. He'd better snap out of this soon, she was thinking. Like her, Finn was starting a new school in September. A kid who finds dusting fascinating isn't going to make many friends. Other kids will run for their lives when they see him coming.

'Anyway,' finished Finn, 'I can't stand here all day chatting about dusting, interesting though it is. I've got work to do.'

He jabbed eagerly upwards with his new cobweb cleaner. In two seconds the web would be wrecked – just wisps of silk on Finn's duster.

Then something happened. Finn's right arm seemed to rebel. It drew back.

'Be obedient. Your destiny is to dust!' Finn told his right arm angrily.

It quivered by his side, still grasping the cobweb cleaner. He grabbed it with his left hand and tried to force it upwards. Finn had a brief wrestling match with himself. But his right arm won. It broke free and slammed down to his side again.

'Botheration!' said Finn. 'Excuse my French.'

Finn looked upward again. There was an epic struggle going on inside his body as the old Finn tried to get the upper hand over Lady Withers' prim, fuss-pot Finn.

'A spider's web is the sign of a slothful servant!' Finn told himself severely.

But the web was perfect, a marvel of spider engineering. And more than that, it had an occupant.

'You're for the chop too,' said Finn. 'Prepare to be dusted to death. *The only good spider is a dead spider.*' But his voice was faltering. He sounded less and less convinced.

There were six tiny eyes in a tower on the spider's back. They stared down at Finn, sparkling like jewels. Eight long legs, as thin as hairs, tested the web for bouciness, as if it was a trampoline. There was a neat white bundle in one corner of the web. An insect wrapped up in a sticky shroud.

'Awww,' said the old Finn. 'You caught something. You clever old thing!'

And, at that moment, Lady Withers lost.

Miss Burgess had guessed right. The Servants' Friend just couldn't compete with Finn's love for his eight-legged friends.

Finn's shoulders naturally relaxed into a slouch. He looked around him with that familiar puzzled frown. 'Why am I holding your titanium hiking stick and tea cup?' he asked Miss Burgess.

Phoebe almost said, 'Because you were going to kill a spider with it.' But she couldn't tell him the truth – it would have been too traumatic. He didn't seem to remember anything about being a cleaning bore and an unbearably smug little prig. Perhaps it was better that way.

He put his hand up to his nose.

'Ugh,' he said, inspecting his fingers. 'Why is my nose so snotty?' He wiped his fingers all over his T-shirt.

Welcome back, bro, thought Phoebe. There was no doubt about it, the old Finn was back.

'That was easy,' decided Phoebe, encouraged. She'd thought Lady Withers would put up more of a fight. It seemed she was a pushover. Phoebe was already making plans for freeing Ruby Dove. If only she could do it – somehow reach back into the past.

Then, as if she was reading Phoebe's mind, Miss Burgess said, 'I think we'll write another letter.'

'It won't work,' said Phoebe. 'She won't write about Ruby. She'll just rave on about your handwriting being rubbish.'

'Not mine she won't,' said Miss Burgess, tight-lipped. 'She wouldn't dare. I got first prize for handwriting at school.'

Phoebe knew that wasn't the point. She understood a bit about Lady Withers. It wasn't only that she wanted Ruby for a servant. It gave her a buzz, putting kids like Ruby down. Making them feel worthless.

'It doesn't matter if your handwriting is perfect!' she tried to explain to Miss Burgess. 'She'll still say it's rubbish. The more perfect it is, the more she'll say it's rubbish. Just to make sure you don't get uppity.'

Miss Burgess shot Phoebe a surprised look. The look said, 'You're more brainy than I thought.'

'Anyway,' said Miss Burgess, 'it doesn't matter what she writes back. She can write what she likes. It's that old postbox I'm interested in. You say that somehow your letters disappear from it? And her replies take their place?'

When she heard it like that, Phoebe realized how crazy it sounded. She'd even starting wondering herself if she was seriously losing her marbles. Her doubts made her yell, even more defiantly, 'That's what happens! Honest. I'm not lying.'

'Do let's keep our voices down!' bellowed Miss Burgess, as if she was addressing a football crowd. That class of tinies she taught must have quaked in their boots every time she opened her mouth. In slightly less ear-splitting tones, she continued, 'We'll post another letter. Then we'll sit and wait and watch what happens.'

'I don't think Finn should go back down there,' whispered Phoebe. 'She's powerful. She might brainwash him again.'

'I doubt it,' said Miss Burgess, glancing over at him. Finn was letting the spider he'd almost dusted to death scuttle all over his hand. He was whispering sweet nothings to it. 'Who's a pretty boy then?'

'She's probably given him up as a bad job,' said Miss Burgess. 'Besides, her power doesn't seem very strong here.'

Phoebe sniffed the air in the Old School kitchen. 'I can't smell her,' she said. 'Not one whiff of lavender.'

'Smell her?'

'You'll know when she's around. There's this lavender smell and this weird jangly noise and –'

Phoebe shivered at the memory. It was all coming back to her now. She couldn't find words to describe that sense of malice she'd felt when she'd collected that last reply. Lady Withers didn't like being challenged. She hated her advice being contradicted. It drove her into a fury. Phoebe was beginning to think they'd escaped very lightly with Finn. The Servants' Friend didn't really care about controlling him. She was probably just practising. But the battle for Ruby Dove was going to bring her out fighting.

Miss Burgess took an old-fashioned fountain pen out of her pocket. 'Do you have any paper?' she asked Phoebe. 'And an envelope?'

She started to write, very slowly, very deliberately, like she did everything. She had beautiful copper-plate handwriting, even better than Ruby Dove's.

How can The Servants' Friend find anything wrong with that? thought Phoebe. But she would. You could bet on it.

'I feel as if I'm sitting a test,' said Miss Burgess, surprised by her own nervousness. 'As if someone's looking over my shoulder!'

'You always feel like that with The Servants' Friend,' said Phoebe. 'Even teachers do. That's how powerful she is.'

Miss Burgess took a long time to write the letter. At last, she finished it and sealed it into the envelope. She wrote *Lady Withers* on the front.

'Did you write to her about Ruby?' asked Phoebe. 'Did you tell her to stop giving Ruby rubbish advice? She might listen to you. I'm only a kid. She doesn't listen to kids.'

But Miss Burgess was busy sticking down the envelope. She didn't seem to hear Phoebe's questions.

'You coming down the garden, Finn?'

Phoebe called over to her brother. 'You don't have to come if you don't want to.'

'I might as well,' said Finn, dragging himself out of a daze. 'I'll look for my zebra spider on the way.' He'd remembered her, now he was back to his old self. The thought of her all alone in her dark matchbox prison tormented him. But he still hadn't give up hope.

Being un-brainwashed had brought back other painful memories too. Memories he could hardly bear – of his ex-hero, Dr Clinton C. Clinton, and the self-righteous smirk on his face as he turned on the hot-water tap.

Don't think about it any more. Right? Finn ordered his disobedient brain. But the whole ghastly scene, everything he'd spied through the window of The Lair, kept trying to re-run itself in his mind.

Finn stood on a chair. He parked his spider back in its web. He did it very gently, so as not to disturb a single thread.

'There,' Finn told the spider. 'I've put you right next to your dinner.' He watched it sink its fangs into its paralysed victim.

'Did you know,' he told Phoebe, 'that spiders inject this stuff into their prey that dissolves all its insides? Then they suck out their dinner. Like a vampire! Except a vampire sucks blood. And dissolved insides would be more like strawberry milkshake. Except not like that really. Because a fly's insides probably don't taste like strawberry milkshake. *Or do they?*' Finn's eyes widened like a mad scientist's. 'I might try a few little experiments!'

'Shut up, Finn,' snapped Phoebe, who felt herself going green. She was beginning to think she preferred Finn when he was addicted to dusting. At least then he wasn't so disgusting.

Miss Burgess bustled to her feet. She grasped her hiking stick in one hand and the envelope in the other. 'Are we ready? Do you want to go to the toilet before we go?' Miss Burgess boomed at Phoebe.

Phoebe shot her a reproachful look. 'For heaven's sake! I'm eleven years old!'

'Sorry,' said Miss Burgess. 'Once a teacher, always a teacher.'

As they were trooping out of the kitchen

door, Miss Burgess suddenly turned back.

'Would you mind if I borrowed the notebook? The one you found in the attic? It's just that I've been interested in old machines ever since I was a girl. There were some threshing machines on our farm that I used to tinker about with.'

What a strange childhood Miss Burgess must have had, thought Phoebe. Sheep wrestling and messing about with threshing machines? No wonder she was a bit weird.

Phoebe shrugged. 'Take it.' The notebook didn't seem very important to her. It didn't make any sense. Even Ruby's jottings in the margins were mysterious. One said, 'Is the pump engine in good repair? Can it supply sufficient water to the garden?' What kind of questions were those? They didn't fit in with what she knew about Ruby's life. What had they got to do with dreams – or dusting?

'I'll treat it with great respect, of course,' said Miss Burgess, picking the notebook up and zipping it into her backpack. Phoebe noticed that she handled it very carefully. As if it was something really rare and precious.

Chapter Eight

On the way down to the old postbox they met Dad. He didn't seem surprised to see Miss Burgess. He didn't even ask them where they were going.

'You know,' he said, scratching his head, 'I still can't figure out our water supply. There must be a maze of secret streams under this moorland.'

'There are,' said Miss Burgess. 'There are underground caves too, deep in the rock.'

'*Wow!*' said Finn, after Dad wandered away. 'Underground caves! Will you show me one? Spiders just love living in underground caves –'

'Finn,' snapped Phoebe. 'We've got more important things to do.'

The closer they got to the postbox, the

more twitchy she felt. Her stomach felt scrunched up, small as a walnut.

'And if you say the word *spider* one more time,' Phoebe threatened him, 'I'm going to pull your head off.'

'Catch you later. I'm off to look for my lost zebra –' said Finn, dodging away just as Phoebe made a grab for him. 'Arachnid!' yelled Finn from the safety of the bushes.

Phoebe let him go. Her hands were shaking too much at the moment. They couldn't pull the head off a dandelion. She shoved them into her pockets. You're a bag of nerves! she scolded herself. It wasn't Finn's fault. He didn't understand how scary The Servants' Friend was. He didn't even know he'd been brainwashed.

Miss Burgess strode boldly forward, whacking rhododendrons out the way with her silvery hiking stick. She didn't seem worried. Or maybe she was just an excellent actress.

What am I doing here? thought Phoebe. I must be crazy! Crazy enough to think she could change history and, somehow, save

Ruby Dove from the evil clutches of Lady Withers, who wanted to ruin a kid's life just so she could keep her castle spick and span. How selfish is that? Miss Burgess was right. Lady Withers couldn't see past Ruby's muscles.

But *I* can see the dream in Ruby's head, thought Phoebe. If only I knew what that dream was.

'So this is the postbox,' said Miss Burgess as they reached the last bit of the old garden wall still standing.

'I definitely smell lavender,' she added, wrinkling her nose. 'It's quite strong.' She bent down. 'Especially close to the ground.'

'That's how it starts,' warned Phoebe. 'Try not to breathe it in or you'll end up polishing dustbins.'

So Lady Withers was here, the old busy-body, the old dream-wrecker. Didn't she *ever* sleep?

'Course she doesn't sleep, she's dead,' Phoebe told herself. Then wished she hadn't. She braced herself for the whole works – creepy janglings, that frosty anger cold enough to turn you to ice crystals, Lady Withers showing her power like a witch doctor rattling his bones.

But it never happened. There was a tiny tinkle – then Mrs Burgess barged in with her booming voice. 'Come out and face us!' she thundered. 'I know you're here!'

Phoebe felt a shiver of panic. But a strange relief as well. Lady Withers was as slippery as a ferret. She ducked and dived, wouldn't answer questions that really mattered. She hid behind criticisms of your handwriting and silly advice about greasing your nose. Now they'd flushed her out into the open. Soon they'd be face to face with The Servants' Friend.

The rhododendron bushes parted. Phoebe felt her heart almost jerk to a stop.

A strange, stooping figure emerged. Its nose came first. A nose that shone softly in the weak sunlight. It wore too-tight jeans that made its legs look like blue pipe cleaners. It had enormous feet, in nerdy leather open-toed sandals.

'Don't tell me that's Lady Withers!' gasped Phoebe, taken aback.

'Of course not,' said Miss Burgess briskly. 'That's my nephew, the famous spider psychologist, Dr Clinton C. Clinton.'

Finn popped up beside them like a jack in the box.

'Don't talk to me about him!' he raged. 'I hate him! He's a secret spider killer. I saw him through the windows of The Lair. He had this big feather duster and he was swishing about with it. And then, and then –' Finn couldn't continue. It was just too upsetting

But it didn't matter. He'd got his message across. Miss Burgess and Phoebe stared at Finn, open-mouthed. Then they stared at each other.

'She's got my nephew!' said Miss Burgess, appalled. 'I don't believe it. He's the last person in the world I'd expect to fall under her influence. Children tell me he's *really cool*!'

'Well, they're lying!' snarled Finn.

That sneaky old Servants' Friend, thought Phoebe. No wonder she wasn't bothering to put on a big, flashy act at the postbox. She didn't need to flaunt her power. She'd already proved what she could do. Phoebe could practically imagine her smug smile.

Dr Clinton whisked a bright yellow duster out of the back pocket of his jeans. He didn't notice the small huddle of spectators talking about him. He seemed in a trance.

'Anything need cleaning round here?' he said into thin air.

He dusted a few rhododendron leaves. He gave the postbox a quick polish. Then slipped his hand inside and took out Miss Burgess's letter.

'She's sent him to fetch her letters,' hissed Miss Burgess.

'Let's follow him,' whispered Phoebe, as Dr Clinton, letter in hand, set off over the moors. 'Then we'll find *her*.'

Miss Burgess seemed about to agree, then changed her mind. 'No, no,' she said. 'It might be dangerous. I've got to do this alone.'

How can someone who practically worships dusting be such a scary and sinister enemy? But Miss Burgess wasn't deceived. She understood now what a tough struggle lay ahead. The Servants' Friend mustn't be underestimated. She wrecked dreams – and lives. And now she'd got her claws into Clinton, Miss Burgess's favourite nephew.

'If she thinks she's getting away with that,' muttered Miss Burgess, 'she's got another think coming!'

Miss Burgess felt very protective towards

Clinton. Others only saw him on TV. He seemed cool and confident – the kind of expert any worried, spider-owning child would turn to in a crisis. Only *she* knew what Dr Clinton C. Clinton was really like. Being brainwashed by a power-mad Victorian agony aunt was something he just didn't need. Not on top of all his other problems.

Phoebe watched Miss Burgess stride away over the moors. Miss Burgess turned back once. 'See you soon!' she bellowed. A startled lapwing tumbled out of the sky.

Phoebe shook her head. 'I don't have a good feeling about this,' she told Finn.

Finn turned to his sister. 'Look, what's going on?' he said. 'Something strange is happening around here. What were you and Miss Burgess muttering about in the kitchen?'

Phoebe sighed. All she could see of Miss Burgess now was her collapsible titanium hiking stick. It glittered once like a star, then it vanished. On the other side of the valley was The Lair, clinging to the cliff like a crouching goblin. It seemed to be waiting for her.

'Finn, I'll tell you in a minute, but right now Miss Burgess and Dr Clinton are heading for

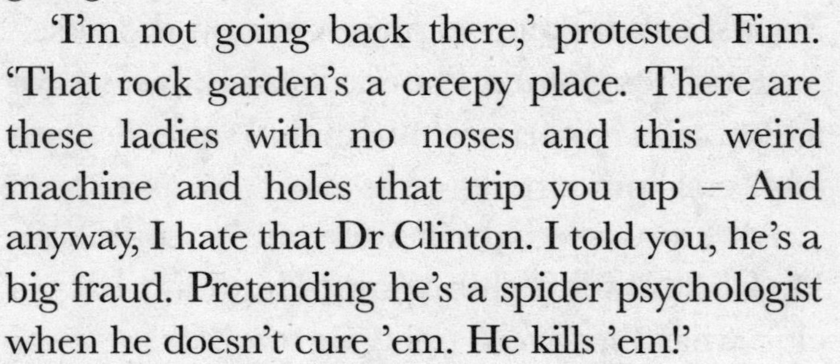

The Lair,' said Phoebe, 'and we should be going with them.'

'I'm not going back there,' protested Finn. 'That rock garden's a creepy place. There are these ladies with no noses and this weird machine and holes that trip you up – And anyway, I hate that Dr Clinton. I told you, he's a big fraud. Pretending he's a spider psychologist when he doesn't cure 'em. He kills 'em!'

'It's not his fault, Finn.'

'Eh?' said Finn, looking bewildered. 'I saw him flush a spider down the sink. With my own eyes!'

'Look, Finn,' said Phoebe patiently, 'I think you've got left behind in this story. I'm going to bring you up to speed.'

As they walked back through the garden, Phoebe told Finn about Lady Withers and Ruby Dove and how he'd been brainwashed, just like his hero Clinton C. Clinton.

Every so often you could hear Finn wail, 'Oh no, I didn't nearly kill a spider? I didn't tidy away my socks? Not in *pairs*?'

How was he ever going to live it down?

But by the time they reached the Old School, Finn had swapped his hatred for Dr

Clinton to Lady Withers. He was itching to rush right over to The Lair. 'I'm going to find her! And I'm going to punch her on the nose!'

'Finn,' explained Phoebe wearily, 'we've got to be a lot smarter than that. We're dealing with evil spirits here.'

All Finn cared about was that he could join Dr Clinton's fan club again. He didn't have a clue what they were up against.

Now his mind skipped off somewhere else. 'This Lady Withers,' asked Finn, 'was she married to Lord Withers, the most famous arachnologist of all time and the author of *Pooter Hunting for Boys*?'

Phoebe searched her memory. 'Yep, she was. Miss Burgess told me. But what's that got to do with anything?'

Finn looked shocked at her ignorance. 'That's a classic book, that is. It's the bible of us spider collectors. I must have read it a hundred times.'

'Not my idea of a good read,' muttered Phoebe. She wasn't really paying attention. She never did when Finn babbled on about spiders. She was thinking about Miss Burgess facing The Servants' Friend all alone.

'I never knew he used to live at The Lair as well,' Finn marvelled. That house seemed to be a magnet for spider enthusiasts.

'And there's a funny thing about Lord Withers,' Finn rambled on. 'It's, like, one of the great unsolved mysteries of the spider world. He was this really shy, gentle spider collector. Right? Everyone liked him. He didn't have any enemies. Anyway, one day in 1875, he was supposed to give a lunchtime talk at the Savoy Hotel in London. The subject was,' said Finn, who could have won *Mastermind* answering questions on his favourite author, '"The Female Black Widow Spider as Cannibal". She scoffs her mate, see,' added Finn helpfully. 'Anyhow, he never turned up. He just disappeared. Like, *vanished off the face of the earth*!'

'*Hmm*,' said Phoebe. This time she was half-listening to what Finn said. Her brain was ticking over. But it didn't make any connections. Not yet . . .

Finn went to his bedroom. He had important work to do: he had to unpair his socks and generally mess the place up.

But Phoebe was restless. She wandered about and found herself up in the shadow-filled attic, sorting once more through the junk. She didn't even know what she was looking for really. She was just killing time.

'Hey!' She'd struck lucky. She'd found another *Arm Oil and Elbow Grease.* She read the date greedily – *August 1880*. 'I haven't got this one!'

She turned feverishly to the back page. Maybe Ruby had written another letter to The Servants' Friend. Maybe they'd printed another reply.

But she never reached the *Answers to Correspondents*. A photo, or rather, half a photo, slipped out of the magazine pages.

As soon as Phoebe looked at it, she felt an icy hand squeeze her heart. It couldn't be, could it?

Phoebe stuffed the copy of *Arm Oil and Elbow Grease* into her pocket. Clutching the torn-off piece of photo, she scrambled back down the attic ladder and raced for her bedroom. Flinging things about, she found the picture of Ruby and fitted the two bits together. Perfect match.

She slumped, breathless, on to her bed. She knew what the whole sentence on the back of the picture said now: Ruby Dove receiving the first prize for polishing, *kindly presented by Lady Withers.*

It was her! That meddler in people's minds. She was on the missing part of the photo. She was standing right next to Ruby, and Ruby had no idea who she really was!

I feel dizzy, thought Phoebe, her head spinning. I don't feel very well.

It was as if The Servants' Friend could reach you, even through her photo.

Don't be stupid, thought Phoebe, forcing herself to turn the picture over. Look at her properly!

Phoebe didn't know what she'd expected. The Servants' Friend was a scrawny little woman. There wasn't a gram of spare flesh on her bones. Her hair was scraped back from her skull into a black lace cap. Her broomstick arms had sharp elbows. Her foxy face had a sharp nose. Her bright, beady eyes were as alert as a crow's. Her dry lips were stretched in a smug, self-righteous smirk.

Phoebe knew what that smirk meant. It meant, '*You're mine now, Ruby Dove.*'

The Servants' Friend was all bones and angles. There was no softness about her. Even her clothes looked stiff. Why were they crow-black? And then Phoebe remembered that, when this picture was taken, she was mourning Lord Withers. That shy, gentle spider collector, who'd vanished off the face of the earth.

Get a grip, Phoebe scolded herself. She's only human. Except she's a *dead* human.

Phoebe had a lot of trouble coping with that fact. She kept forgetting that the business between Ruby Dove and The Servants' Friend wasn't happening now, in the present, but 120 years in the past.

Phoebe was recovering a bit now. She didn't feel so trembly. It somehow gave her power to see The Servants' Friend face to face, as if she'd finally pinned her down.

'I've found out who you really were,' muttered Phoebe to herself. 'And now I know what you look like.' It felt, at last, as if she'd got an advantage.

She knew the reason for those strange

jangling noises too. Lady Withers had a big bunch of keys on her belt. The keys to the castle, thought Phoebe. Typical. It was just like her to be in charge of every key to every door in The Lair. She probably kept her flannel underwear folded up in drawers full of lavender. That would be typical of her too. Every time she took a step, lavender sprigs were scattered from her knickers.

Phoebe looked again at the picture of Ruby Dove. 'I'll fix her, I promise,' she told Ruby.

Phoebe zipped the picture of Lady Withers into her coat pocket.

'I'm not leaving you alone with Ruby,' she told her, 'I'm not taking any chances. Even if it is only your photo.'

Never underestimate the power of The Servants' Friend. Phoebe had learned that lesson very well.

She shrugged on her coat, then went and rapped on Finn's bedroom door. 'Finn!' she yelled.

He was inside, flicking through his favourite book, *Pooter Hunting for Boys*. He practically knew it by heart. His pet collection was in immaculate order again. Every shoebox and tank was neatly labelled – their occupants happily doing what spiders do. Those who trapped their victims in webs were spinning. Those who liked to hide in dark holes were lurking. The rest of Finn's room looked like a rubbish dump. There was a red football sock dangling from the lamp shade. But that was all right. It reassured Phoebe that Finn was really back to normal.

'I know Miss Burgess said stay here,' said Phoebe, 'but I think we should go and give her some back-up. Help her save her nephew from The Servants' Friend.'

'I'm right behind you!' said Finn eagerly. If Dr Clinton C. Clinton needed rescuing, then he could count on Finn, his loyal fan.

'I had a little accident with his photo,' Finn confessed to Phoebe, looking at the picture he'd shredded and scattered in confetti-sized pieces all over the floor. 'Do you think he'd mind signing another one?'

Chapter Nine

All the way to The Lair, Finn looked for the matchbox containing his lost zebra spider. He wasn't about to give up. Spiders can last for six months without a square meal.

Phoebe had the picture of Lady Withers in her pocket. And now she had a picture of her in her mind – something to focus her anger on.

'You think you're so *right,* don't you?' muttered Phoebe. 'Don't you ever think you're wrong about *anything*?'

One look into those cold, beady eyes would tell you the answer to that. There was no doubt in those eyes. None at all.

With sudden alarm, Phoebe noticed that Finn's nose looked suspiciously shiny. 'Finn!'

she said sharply. 'You've been putting best butter on your nose again. I thought you'd given that up!'

Finn looked shifty. 'It's just what I do before I go out,' he said with a shrug. 'Spray my armpits, gel my hair, grease my nose . . . It's no big deal. I'm not being brainwashed. Honest!'

'What do you think of dusting?' demanded Phoebe, jabbing a finger in his chest. 'Quick! Answer my question!'

'I hate dusting!' cried Finn, with feeling. 'I mean, what's the point of it? There must be more to life! You dust. Then more dust comes. Then you dust, then more dust comes. Then you dust –'

'OK, OK,' said Phoebe testily. 'You can stop now. I'm convinced. I just thought Lady Withers might have nobbled you again, that's all.'

'No way!' said Finn indignantly. 'Although, actually,' he confessed, half-embarrassed, 'I might carry on buttering my nose. My nose was all rough and scaly before, you know, where I picked it. And now it's lovely and soft and smooth,' said Finn, giving his nose an affectionate rub. 'As smooth as a baby's bum. I'd recommend best butter to anyone. Just a dab on your nose each morning in the bathroom.'

'Shut up, Finn,' said Phoebe. 'Don't tell me what you do in the bathroom. I don't want to know.'

'There's an interesting spider that lives in bathrooms,' Finn pointed out. 'The Australian redback spider. It's got this *really* painful bite. It lurks under the toilet seat and, just when you've settled your bare bum on the loo and got comfy and you're peacefully reading a comic or something it shoots out and –'

'I don't want to know that either!'

They reached the rock garden. More bits had fallen off the dancing ladies. One seemed to have lost a leg.

'Listen to this,' said Finn. He stopped by a drill hole and did a wild stamping dance with his boots.

'*Ommmmm, ommmm, ommmm.*' Low notes came rushing up from deep underground, like belches rumbling up from a giant's belly.

'See,' said Finn. 'It's hollow down there. Miss Burgess said there were caves.'

'I told you,' Phoebe interrupted, 'we haven't got time to go looking for spiders in caves.'

'No, I know,' said Finn. 'I'm not a complete idiot! I need to find Dr Clinton first. My hissing cockroach needs some therapy. I think he's depressed. He hasn't hissed for days.'

'I thought Dr Clinton was a spider specialist,' said Phoebe.

'He's like me,' said Finn proudly. 'Some spider fanatics think eight legs good, six legs bad. But we don't. We're interested in other bugs as well.'

'Finn,' Phoebe reminded him, 'he's not going to be interested in anything, except dusting and cleaning.'

Unless, of course, Miss Burgess had already released him from Lady Withers' influence. But somehow, Phoebe doubted that. She guessed that even Miss Burgess, who could wrestle sheep single-handed, was going to have her work cut out.

They found Miss Burgess peering in through one of the tall, leaded windows of The Lair.

'Chop, chop!' she boomed briskly, clapping her hands as if she was shooing a crowd of five-year-olds into class. 'Didn't I tell you not to follow me? Scamper back where you came from, quickly and quietly!'

Phoebe gave her a long-suffering look. Miss Burgess sighed. 'I'm doing it again, aren't I? Old habits die hard.'

Sometimes, Phoebe thought there were some similarities between Miss Burgess and The Servants' Friend. They were both bossy-boots for a start. But there was one Big Difference, which meant that, deep down, Miss Burgess wasn't like The Servants' Friend at all. Miss Burgess could take a hint. She could take advice, even from an eleven-year-old kid. Lady Withers never, ever took advice, especially from kids. She just laid down the law.

Miss Burgess stood squarely in front of the window. A sudden ray of sunlight lit up the stained glass. It turned her carroty frizz to spun gold.

'He's in there,' she told them, in a grim but determined voice. 'But he's locked all the doors. I've hammered on that big oak front door. I've rapped on this window. Either he can't hear, or he's pretending not to.'

She unslung her backpack and began ferreting in it.

'We've got to find a way in,' she said. Her

voice sounded deadly serious. 'Lady Withers is in there all right. This place is her HQ, the centre of her power.'

Phoebe pressed her nose to the leaded panes. She was looking in at the library, lined with row upon row of sombre books. There wasn't a speck of dirt anywhere. The dark furniture shone like black ice in car headlights. Dr Clinton C. Clinton, world-famous spider psychologist and TV personality, had been doing the polishing. There were six cans of Mr Gleam on a shelf. They were the giant economy size. Neatly lined up next to them were ten cans of Doom!, instant death to spiders. Much more efficient than flushing them down the loo.

Finn would go mad if he saw those, thought Phoebe. One quick squirt and a spider turned as shrivelled and black as a tea leaf. Too late. Finn had shouldered her aside. He'd seen Dr Clinton's cleaning aids.

'We've got to do something!' he said wildly. Apart from the danger to spiders, if anyone saw those cans, especially some snooping reporter, Dr Clinton's career would be ruined.

'Where is he?' said Phoebe. 'I can't even see him.' Then she spotted him.

Dr Clinton was sitting, stooped over, on a high stool at a tall, old-fashioned desk. There was a big bunch of keys on the desk.

They're *her* keys! thought Phoebe. The same keys as in the photo.

She turned round to tell Miss Burgess, but Miss Burgess had taken the old notebook out of her backpack. She was busy studying one of the pages.

'Finn, come over here a minute,' she said urgently. 'Read this for me. Your eyes are better than mine.'

Phoebe couldn't keep her own eyes away from that window. She peered in again. It was hard to see through the gloom. Dr Clinton was writing something. He had Miss Burgess's letter open on the desk beside him and a fresh piece of paper in front of him. He had a wooden pen with a nib and an ink bottle. And the ink he was using was –

'*Purple*,' breathed Phoebe.

Her face was bone-white. She turned away from the window.

'Miss Burgess!' Miss Burgess looked up from

the notebook. 'It's *him* writing the letters,' Phoebe told her in a trembling voice. 'It was him all the time.'

'I know,' said Miss Burgess. 'I've just realized that too. She's using my nephew as her servant – to clean the house, to write her replies, to run her errands. How dare she? He's even writing in her handwriting! She's totally taken over control of his mind.'

Just at that moment, a familiar smell came wafting through the ventilation brick at the side of the window.

Dr Clinton C. Clinton wasn't alone. She was in there with him, in the very same room, telling him what to write.

'Come on,' urged Finn. 'Let's go into those caves.'

'Finn!' Phoebe almost shrieked. 'What's the matter with you? I told you, there isn't time to –'

'No, no,' Miss Burgess interrupted her. 'That's the other way in. Through the tunnels and caves under this garden. There's a map in the notebook. There should be an entrance,' she said, consulting the notebook again, 'somewhere round here.'

Finn was already busy looking.

'But I don't understand. Who did the notebook belong to?' asked Phoebe desperately. 'And why did Ruby write in it?'

'It belonged to her poor father, Philip Dove. What a genius that man was! Musician, engineer, landscape gardener. His talents were never-ending! He just never had any good luck, that's all. But I haven't got time to explain now. We have to get into The Lair. My nephew was always a brainy lad. I knew he'd go far. But now he thinks it's his destiny to dust. I'm not having that! And besides,' added Miss Burgess anxiously, 'he's got enough personal problems as it is, without having The Servants' Friend poking her big nose into his life.'

'Problems? What personal problems?' said Finn, sharp as a tack. 'I've been on Dr Clinton's web site. I've visited it 143 times, and it doesn't say anything about personal problems. It hasn't got anything to do with those nerdy seaside sandals he wears, has it?' asked Finn, with a sudden flash of inspiration. 'Because even I was a bit shocked about *them*.'

Whoops, thought Miss Burgess. How did he guess? Me and my big mouth.

She went immediately into teacher mode. 'Who said we could have all this talking?' she thundered. 'Chop, chop, children, we've got work to do.'

Her booming voice found somewhere hollow to bounce around in. Echoes came back from under the ground, *'Work to do, work to do.'*

'Hey!' said Finn, parting some ferns and staring into a hole as wide as a well. 'I think I've found the way in.'

Chapter Ten

It wasn't exactly like potholing. The way in was no problem – there was even a long iron ladder to help you climb down. And under the stone garden of The Lair you didn't need torches. The tunnels and caves were dimly lit with green, wavy shadows, as sunshine squeezed past the ferns and down through the holes in the rock. It was eerie. Like walking under the sea.

'*Wow!*' breathed Finn, looking around. 'This is magic!'

They were in a small underground cave, about the size of Finn's bedroom. Crystals glittered in the craggy folds of the roof. Stalagmites rose from the floor like a forest of melted candles.

'According to Philip Dove's map, we go left,'

said Miss Burgess, stopping under a shaft of light to check the notebook, 'into a tunnel.'

They didn't have to crawl. The tunnel was big enough to stand up in, except for Miss Burgess who had to stoop. Water dripped down the slimy walls. Weird luminous fungi glowed yellow and orange and bright green.

The tunnel opened out into another cave, much grander this time. It seemed higher than a church. You couldn't even see the roof. It was lost up there in the darkness.

'Who made this place?' asked Phoebe in an awed voice. 'All these tunnels? It's like a secret world down here.'

'Most of it's natural,' said Miss Burgess, without looking round. 'Made by underground streams forcing their way through the rock. But some of it's manmade, by Philip Dove. He made those holes you can see in the cave walls. Some of them go all the way up to the surface. He had the streams dammed so he could work safely down here without being drowned.'

'What was he working on?' asked Phoebe. She wanted to know all about Ruby's father.

'Rock music,' said Miss Burgess shortly. 'He

had his musician's hat on when he was working down here. And his engineer's hat probably. Because he had to do lots of drilling and blasting through rock.'

'But I thought you said Ruby was an orphan? And anyway, what happened to her mum?'

It wasn't the time to pester Miss Burgess with questions. There was only one thing on her mind – getting inside The Lair to rescue her nephew. The coming battle with The Servants' Friend was making her more and more jittery. She wasn't sure how to tackle a power-crazed Victorian agony aunt. She wasn't at all sure she could win. She took a deep breath and strode ahead. 'It's not far now. According to this map we come up in the cellar.'

Phoebe followed her. But Finn lagged behind. He'd seen something. All his spider-hunting instincts sparked into life. Even though they were on an emergency rescue mission, he just couldn't help himself.

'Wow!' he gasped for the second time since they'd entered the caves.

Gently, he scooped up something from the

cave floor. It was very fragile. To a non-spider-fancier it looked like a black, shrivelled claw with eight fingers. But Finn knew different. The thing was light, as light as a skeleton leaf. He would have to be careful. It could easily crumble into dust.

It was the cast-off cuticle of a moulting spider. Finn had never seen one this size. And, by shedding its skin, this spider had grown from a very big spider into an even bigger spider.

'I've never seen anything like this before!' marvelled Finn, cradling the football-sized cuticle. 'This spider must be a monster!'

'Finn!' Phoebe's anxious warnings came echoing back down the tunnel. 'Where are you? Hurry up. Don't get lost!'

Cupping his precious find in both hands, Finn followed the sound of her voice.

'I'm going to show this to Dr Clinton,' he thought.

In his excitement, he forgot that Dr Clinton was no longer the spider's best friend. If Dr Clinton saw a spider, his first impulse wouldn't be to sort out its problems. It would be to give it a quick blast of Doom!, then flush it away

down the loo. In fact, Finn and his hero had nothing at all in common now, except for their shiny, Rudolph-the-Reindeer noses.

'Botheration,' said Miss Burgess.

They'd come to a dead end. At the top of some stone steps the way to the cellar was blocked by a great stone slab. 'This shouldn't be here, not according to Philip Dove's map,' she told Phoebe.

Miss Burgess spat on her hands. 'Keep well clear!' With her sheep-wrestling muscles she heaved up the slab and slid it to one side.

'Wow!' said Finn, impressed. He looked at his own weedy muscles. I'm going to have to work out, he decided. Sometimes he didn't have the strength to pop open a bag of cheese and onion crisps.

'I'm a bit out of puff,' apologized Miss Burgess. 'I haven't done that kind of thing since I was a girl. Although I do toss the caber at weekends,' she added, 'just to keep in shape.'

Phoebe sighed. Were all teachers this weird? Her own seemed quite normal. Perhaps they went wild after they retired.

They were inside The Lair.

'There should be a light here somewhere,'

said Miss Burgess, searching the wall for a switch. 'Ah, I've found it.'

Immediately the cellar was bathed in a dim, yellow glow. It was full of dusty bottles of wine. Old cobwebs, stiff with glittering bits of beetle, hung like chainmail from the roof beams. Lady Withers obviously hadn't sent her servant, Dr Clinton, to clean down here yet. She'd get round to it, after he'd done all the floors above.

'Blast!' cursed Miss Burgess, forgetting the sensitive ears of children. 'You can't rely on these old maps.'

The way out of the cellar was blocked too, by an iron grille. It was padlocked into place. Miss Burgess rattled it, put her shoulder up against it and shoved. But even her superior strength couldn't shift it.

She tried forcing the padlock. She used her titanium hiking stick and teacup as a lever. It bent like a liquorice stick.

'Huh!' said Miss Burgess in disgust. She hurled it away. Why had she believed those tempting advertising slogans? . . . *'This stick will last much longer than you do.'* . . . *'This stick will survive when you don't.'*

'I can get through there,' said Finn.

He put down his cast-off spider cuticle. He sucked in his ribs until his stomach kissed his spine. He slid between the iron bars, then slid back again. 'Easy peasy,' he said proudly. He was glad now he'd never worked out. Any boy with muscles bigger than jelly beans would never have made it through that gap.

'I think I know where the key to this padlock is,' said Phoebe. 'You know when we looked in the library window just now? That big bunch of keys on the desk?'

It was bound to be one of them. Lady Withers would have the keys to every lock in The Lair – to every store cupboard and china cabinet and desk drawer. Even to this rusty grille deep in the cellar. She was that kind of busybody. She had to be in charge.

'Wait,' said Miss Burgess, looking worried. 'Finn shouldn't go up there on his own –'

But Finn was already on his way upstairs. He called back over his shoulder, 'Mind my spider skin. That's something really special, that is!'

The fourth door Finn opened was the library. He should have known anyway. You just had to follow your nose. That smell of lavender crept along corridors. It seemed to swirl round your ankles like the incoming tide. He'd only stopped once as he was passing the dark tapestries and gloomy family portraits. It was to look up at a huge painting of Lord Withers, that well-known author of *Pooter Hunting for Boys* and brilliant arachnologist. Finn gave a respectful salute. Lord Withers was number two on his list of heroes.

Funny, thought Finn, as he gawped upwards at the portrait. The people in the other portraits looked stand-offish and snooty, as if they had bad smells under their noses. But Lord Withers just looked – really scared.

Dr Clinton didn't seem to hear Finn come in. He was still perched on his high stool, hunched over the desk. Every so often he dipped the nib in the purple ink. Finn spotted the keys. That's what he'd come for.

'Just grab 'em and run,' the sensible side of his brain told him. But being so close to his number one hero was such a big thrill . . .

Wonder if he's got any signed photos in that desk, thought Finn. He might even have one of his T-shirts. The ones he gave away free

during his TV Show, which said on the front, 'Don't stand ON spiders!' and on the back, 'Stand UP for 'em!'

Strangely, that lavender smell didn't bother Finn much, even though it was really strong now. He must have got used to it. He edged sidewards like a crab. He could see right over Dr Clinton's shoulder now, as he scribbled away.

Dr Clinton was clearly Lady Withers' servant through and through. He was writing down her thoughts, in her writing too, as if she was guiding his mind and his hand.

Finn glimpsed a few words of Lady Withers' reply to Miss Burgess.

'Deplorable handwriting, shocking impatience, importance of flannel knickers –'

Oh dear, thought Finn, with sudden dread. I've forgotten to put mine on.

He felt slightly woozy. His head was spinning. He was rapidly forgetting why he was here. With a superhuman effort, he reached out to grab the keys, but found his finger running along the underneath of the desk.

'*Tut, tut,*' clucked Finn, inspecting his finger. 'A speck of dust! That shouldn't be there.'

From somewhere behind the red velvet curtains came a satisfied crackling sound, as if of stiff skirts rustling. Finn seemed to be a pushover. The Servants' Friend didn't even have to try hard. She was only using about one per cent of her real powers. A scrawny little pipsqueak servant like Finn wasn't much use to her. She had her eye on Miss Burgess – *she* was big and strong. She could do all the heavy work. She reminded Miss Withers of another servant, Ruby Dove who, long ago, had escaped from her clutches.

Finn reached for a can of Mr Gleam.

At that moment, Dr Clinton lifted his head. He didn't move from his high stool, as if an invisible ball and chain kept him there. But his eyes were full of such pleading despair that Finn was shocked back to his senses.

'What am I doing?' he cried, yanking back his hand as if the can of Mr Gleam was white-hot. In that instant, he fought off all thoughts of dusting and flannel knickerbockers. 'I'll be back,' he told Dr Clinton.

He grabbed the keys and hared off down

the corridors, past the portrait of poor Lord Withers, still cowering up there on the wall.

Phoebe was weak with relief to see him. 'Was *she* in the library? Did she try to stop you taking the keys?'

'She was in there somewhere,' said Finn. 'I felt her – she tried to mess up my mind. I smelled her. But I didn't see her.'

Sneaky as ever, thought Phoebe as Finn tried the likeliest keys in the lock. Fighting The Servants' Friend was like fighting a shadow. You could never land a good punch.

'That's the one!' cried Finn, as he found the right key and the iron grille creaked open.

'Take one of these,' said Miss Burgess. She got three hankies out of her cardie pocket. 'Cover your nose to keep out the lavender smell from her lavender knickers.'

Finn frowned at the lacy borders round the hankies. 'They're a bit *girly,* aren't they?'

'They're tatted,' Miss Burgess informed him sternly as they hurried to the library. 'Tatting is a hobby of mine, along with caber tossing. It's most restful. It took me six months to tat that border. Now that's more useful than watching TV, isn't it?'

Finn opened his mouth to protest, then shut it. They were up to their necks in a crisis. His views about tatting versus telly-watching would have to wait until later.

'That's Lord Withers on the wall,' Finn said.

Phoebe threw a glance upwards – but all she could see was a blurred, frightened face.

Chapter Eleven

They burst into the library like the US Marines, with tatted hankies held to their noses.

The lavender smell wasn't the only thing that hit them. The Servants' Friend's cold fury at their interference was so strong that it seemed almost solid – like running into an ice wall.

'Clinton!' cried Miss Burgess.

Dr Clinton looked round. His dull eyes showed no recognition.

'Clinton, it's me, Auntie Flossie!' Miss Burgess appealed to his bent back. He'd shrugged her off, picked up his pen and resumed the task Lady Withers had given him.

Even in this emergency, Finn's butterfly brain marvelled again at Dr Clinton's bony white feet in those leather sandals. He'd also noticed the fact that Miss Burgess's first name was Flossie. He stored it away to laugh at later.

'Right! She's had it now!' cried Miss Burgess in most unteacher-like tones. 'Where is that woman? She's messed us about long enough! I'm going to sort her out!' She pulled up the sleeves of her cardie to show brawny arms.

The crackling of a stiff dress came again from behind the red velvet curtains. It sounded like a raging fire. Lady Withers showed herself for the first time. She glided out from behind the curtains as if she were on wheels. Phoebe gasped. She looked exactly like she did in the photo – sharp elbows, sharp face, sharp nose, and those bright but pitiless eyes.

'Where is she?' hissed Miss Burgess.

'There! There!' cried Phoebe, through her hankie. 'Right in front of us. Can't you see her?'

'No,' said Finn.

'No.' Miss Burgess shook her head, bewildered. She forgot about protecting herself with the tatted hankie. It stayed screwed up in her fist.

Dr Clinton wasn't going to answer. He daren't look up. He had his head down, scribbling like a maniac. *'Flannel knickerbockers, don't stoop, disgraceful handwriting, grease your nose, dust, dust, dust, dust, dust, dust –'*

Phoebe had only turned away for an instant. But when she turned back, The Servants' Friend's shape began to dissolve, like a rippling reflection in a pond. Her malice hung in the air, as sharp and real as an axe. But her body was slowly fading away.

'No you don't!' cried Phoebe. She concentrated fiercely. 'I know what you look like! You can't hide from me! I want to talk to you about Ruby Dove! I want some straight answers!'

The power of her mind seemed to make Lady Withers visible. She came into focus again, the fuzzy edges firmed up. She wriggled about, like a worm caught on a hook. But she couldn't escape.

Phoebe tried fumbling in her pocket. She was going to show the others the photo. She thought, If they know what she looks like, they'll be able to see her too.

But every time she let her thoughts slip

away, even a fraction, from The Servants' Friend, that black crow-like figure started to shake and shiver. If she didn't watch it, it would melt away completely until there was nothing left but the smirk.

Why had Miss Burgess suddenly gone quiet? Phoebe couldn't turn her head to look. She had to keep her eyes fixed like lasers on The Servants' Friend. Why didn't Lady Withers look worried? Her greedy little shark eyes shone with self-satisfaction, as if she'd just pulled off a really sneaky trick.

Then Miss Burgess spoke. 'I don't think Clinton's done a very good job on that sideboard. I should be able to see my reflection in it.'

A quiver of shock went straight through Phoebe's body. 'Not Miss Burgess!' her brain screamed at her.

In that split second everything fell apart. Her mind seemed to break up like a shattered car windscreen. She let the hankie drop from her nose. Lady Withers' body was slipping away. It was becoming transparent – you could see right through her like a shop window.

Phoebe's eyes glazed over. Her mouth

opened. 'My destiny is to dust. My destiny is to dust. My –'

'Quite right too!' interrupted Miss Burgess, passing her a duster, then pointing to the bookshelves. 'You can start on those volumes of the *Encyclopaedia Britannica* A to E. They need a good clean.'

Phoebe moved obediently to obey. Finn, his nose still smothered in lacy hankie, swept the room with a panicky, horrified gaze. He was the only one left! All the others had become cleaning robots with brains full of nothing but Mr Gleam and extra-thick bleach and Fade-away-fast stain remover. They were all busy doing Lady Withers' bidding. They seemed to have forgotten about him.

But Lady Withers hadn't. She never neglected details. Even a flea-sized servant is better than no servant, she was thinking. She hadn't come back from beyond the grave to do her own cleaning.

Finn couldn't see her. But he could feel her circling round. She wasn't in a murderous rage any more. She had successfully crushed the biggest challenges to her power – Miss Burgess and Phoebe. Those two impudent interferers had really made her see red. She could afford to take her time now. Finn was no contest. She was playing with him like a cat with a mouse.

Terrified, Finn backed up to Dr Clinton's desk. He was all on his own. Miss Burgess and Phoebe were clucking like hens, flicking dusters about. Dr Clinton just carried on feverishly writing, covering pages and pages with the same frightful four-letter word – *dust*. As if, left to himself while Lady Withers was busy dealing with Finn, that was all he could find in his head.

Where is she? She was very close – Finn could smell her, even through his hankie. Her crackling skirts sounded as loud as gunshot. Feeling himself cornered, he crashed into the desk. Dr Clinton didn't look up. But page one of Lady Withers' reply to Miss Burgess floated to the floor.

Without knowing what he was doing, Finn caught it one-handed. A few lines leaped out, fixed themselves into his frantic brain.

How dare you question our advice to Ruby Dove or our actions regarding your nephew! We will not be questioned! Your impertinent manner is quite shocking! We are consumed with rage! Wear flannel knickerbockers at all times, especially when ice skating.

Consumed with rage? thought Finn desperately. About a few questions? It doesn't take much to wind *her* up! The Servants' Friend seemed to be very touchy. Anyone who questioned her advice was impertinent. She disapproved of almost everything except dusting. She was always complaining about being shocked and disgusted. A little light came on in Finn's brain. Disgusting other people was one of his greatest talents . . .

I'll shock her, thought Finn. I'll shock her like she's never been shocked before.

'Excuse me,' said Finn, grabbing the pen and a sheet of paper from his hero. Dr Clinton didn't try and stop him. With no writing materials, he just slumped at the desk as if he'd been switched off. Frowning in thought, Finn began scratching away.

It's hard work writing a letter while holding a hankie over your nose. Finn had to let go of the hankie. It was the ideal time for The Servants' Friend to pounce. Finn couldn't see her but she was prowling about very close, looking for a way into his mind. One blast of that strong lavender scent to make his head reel. Then, bingo, she'd be inside his brain like a wolf spider catching a fly, giving him sinister advice, telling him that dusting was the answer to all his dreams.

But she missed her chance. She held back. She'd noticed Finn's nose was well greased. Perhaps she thought there was no need for tough tactics, that Finn was already at her beck and call, obediently writing her letters.

'Do we never fail?' The Servants' Friend asked herself smugly. She answered her own question. 'No, we never do!'

Except for that time with Ruby Dove, when events were beyond her control. But she preferred not to think about that.

Finn finished his letter. He waved it about in the air to dry the ink. Miss Burgess and Phoebe didn't even look round. They had dusted XYZ, the last encyclopaedia, and now they were moving on to Poetry.

'Where are you?' said Finn to empty air. He still couldn't see her, but the room was full of her powerful presence. She seemed to be –

waiting. With one hand, Finn slapped the hankie back on his nose.

He put his piece of paper on the desk. Dr Clinton didn't even raise his head. But Finn knew Lady Withers was a nosy parker. He backed off and heard her stiff skirt rattle as she bustled up to investigate.

Finn's letter, headed *Dear Servants' Friend,* seemed to flutter as if the breeze had caught it, even though there wasn't a whisper of wind in the room. There was a pause. Finn stared very hard at the place where Lady Withers must be standing. Was the atmosphere thicker there? Could he see a bulging shape wobbling in thin air, like a globule of oil in a lava lamp?

Suddenly things happened very fast. Finn's letter was hurled to the floor. He saw it jerk about, crinkling and crumpling, as if someone was stamping on it. Then, before Finn's horrified gaze, little black button-up shoes began to appear. They were giving Finn's letter a good trampling. It was Lady Withers materializing from the feet up. And she seemed to be really mad.

Her dress appeared, like someone sketching

her in jet black ink. Her headless body booted Finn's letter into the far corner. Her sharp elbows were pumping up and down like fury.

Finn had shocked her all right. Reading his letter had driven her demented. Lady Withers, so used to controlling other people, was totally out of control.

There was her scraggy neck. Her face appeared out of order. Her sharp nose came first, quivering with indignation. She had never been so offended in her whole life, or death. The impertinence! The vulgarity! The impolite questions! Even if she could speak, there were no words strong enough to express her disgust.

As her face appeared, twisted with ferocious anger, things speeded up even more. Her normally chalk-white features turned several shades of pink. She was heating up like a hot water tank, her temperature rapidly rising from chilly to warm to roasting. She was boiling!

As Finn watched, appalled, The Servants' Friend's face glowed bright red. It pulsed on and off, on and off, like a fire-engine light. She was going to explode!

With a terrific whoosh, she went up in

flames. The Servants' Friend spontaneously combusted with sheer outrage. She just couldn't deal with Finn's letter. It had made her, literally, blazing mad.

There was a quick furious fire. For five seconds it snarled and spat like a tiger. Then, just as quickly, it went out. Black smoke billowed round the library. Finn coughed, his eyes smarted. He wafted the smoke away. The carpet near the desk was scorched in a neat black circle. In the middle of it was a heap of grey ashes. And in the middle of that, a pair of black button-up shoes. Then before Finn's eyes, they too dissolved into dust.

In the garden of the Old School, among the dark rhododendrons, something else was happening. No one saw it. Phoebe's dad didn't discover it until two days later. But, at the exact moment that The Servants' Friend self-ignited, the last bit of garden wall crumbled. The cast-iron postbox smashed like glass into a thousand sharp pieces. There would be no more letters exchanged between the present and the past.

'What am I doing with this duster?' boomed Miss Burgess.

Finn shook his head. He was still in a daze.

'What happened?' asked Phoebe. 'Where's The Servants' Friend?'

Finn, still speechless, nodded towards the heap of cold, grey dust on the carpet.

He found some words. 'I wrote her a letter,' he said in a stunned voice. 'And she read it. And she got really mad! She just spontaneously combusted. Puff! She went up in smoke!'

'A spirit can't spontaneously combust,' quibbled Phoebe. She didn't trust The Servants' Friend. She was as cunning as a trap-door spider.

'Well, *she* did,' protested Finn. 'And anyway,' he continued, 'it happens with people. It's a scientific fact. This woman in America combusted, just sitting there watching telly! And all they found was her slippers.'

'I think she's really gone,' said Miss Burgess, heaving a grateful sigh. They stood in a solemn circle round the remains of The Servants' Friend. 'She can't make people's lives a misery any more, thanks to you, Finn.'

'I beat her, didn't I?' marvelled Finn. He sounded surprised.

Dr Clinton C. Clinton climbed shakily down from his high stool. His big sandalled feet plonked down on what had been Lady Withers and ground her into the carpet. He looked around him, as if seeing the library for the first time.

'Auntie Flossie, what are you doing here?' He ignored Phoebe and Finn, turning his back on them, as if they were invisible.

Finn thought that was a bit strange, but he was too busy laughing at Miss Burgess's first name. Now the danger was over he needed a good giggle.

'It's a long story, Clinton,' Miss Burgess told her nephew. 'Let's have a cup of tea first, shall we?'

'Wait a minute,' said Phoebe. She sounded upset. 'I never asked her about Ruby Dove. And now it's too late.'

With The Servants' Friend gone, the door to the past seemed firmly shut.

There's still the old postbox though, she reminded herself. 'I'm going to write Ruby a letter,' she said out loud. 'There's no one to open it now. Maybe it'll work. Maybe she'll get it.'

Miss Burgess looked concerned. 'I think you should leave well alone,' she said bluntly. 'We shouldn't go meddling in history.'

Phoebe was hurt. 'But I'm not going to write horrible letters. I'm going to be a real friend and give her *proper* advice, not like that rubbish advice Lady Withers gave her.'

'No good will come of it,' warned Miss Burgess. She could feel it in her bones.

Finn sidled up to Dr Clinton, who still looked groggy. 'Hi, I'm Finn. I'm your number one fan,' said Finn with a grin like a piranha. 'Got any signed photos?'

Dr Clinton seemed alarmed. '*Err, err*,' he stuttered, backing away. He was squirming with distress. He looked as if, faced with his biggest fan, he wanted to run away, screaming, and hide in a cupboard.

What's up with him? thought Finn. Where was that confident, super-cool chap who charmed you every week on telly? Finn knew his hero had been through a traumatic time, but he still felt a bit let down.

'I'm afraid,' whispered Miss Burgess out the side of her mouth, 'that he's wonderful with spiders but useless with people. He hasn't got a clue. That's one of the personal problems I was telling you about.'

'But he's so smooth on telly!' protested Finn.

They were talking about Dr Clinton as if he wasn't there. But he didn't seem to mind. He just put his head down and fidgeted.

'That's talking to a camera,' explained Miss Burgess. 'He can do that. But when it comes to talking to real people he comes over all peculiar. He's so shy he's like a shambling idiot!'

That's a bit strong, thought Phoebe. But Dr Clinton nodded sadly, as if it was all true.

Then Finn's ever-active brain did a hop and a skip. He'd remembered something brilliant. The battle with The Servants' Friend had pushed it right out of his mind. It was something his hero, Dr Clinton, would find fascinating. Maybe it would make him more chatty.

'I've got something to show you!' said Finn to Dr Clinton, 'but I left it down in the cellar. I'll just nip back and get it.'

He dashed off before anyone could stop him. He hoped his cast-off spider cuticle was still in one piece. The spider who shed it must have been a bit of a beast. You'd need a pooter the size of a fire extinguisher to catch him.

'What's been going on?' asked Dr Clinton, talking to the sideboard so he didn't have to speak to anyone face to face. He dimly remembered arriving at his new house and doing some unpacking. But after that, it was all a blank.

Miss Burgess took a deep breath. How to tell him that his mind had been taken over by a rabid Victorian agony aunt who'd just been reduced to a pile of dust? It would need all her teacher's skills to make him understand.

'Well,' began Miss Burgess very slowly and clearly, as if she was talking to a class of tiny tots and not to a brainy boffin, 'pay attention, Clinton. It was like this . . .'

Chapter Twelve

If anyone else but Aunt Flossie had told him that tale, Dr Clinton would have said, 'You can't expect me to believe that load of old claptrap.' Only he probably wouldn't have said it to their face. He would have told the table or the bookshelves instead. But now he just shook his head in a wondering way and shuffled shyly about.

Doesn't he have *anything* to say? thought Phoebe.

On telly he was sparky and full of bounce. He had bags of personality. But in real life he seemed unbearably drippy and droopy. He had as much bounce as a beanbag. As much get-up-and-go as a sea slug. How could he be so different?

Miss Burgess wasn't surprised. She knew

what her nephew was like in private when the cameras stopped filming.

He hasn't improved, she thought sadly. If anything, he's got worse.

He just couldn't cope with people, especially ladies. In ladies' company he became a quivering wreck. Particularly if he couldn't talk about spiders.

He'll never get a girlfriend, Miss Burgess had long ago decided. What modern girl wants to chat about spiders at a romantic candle-lit dinner? And, of course, there was his other little problem. But that wasn't his fault. He'd been born like that.

'My brother Finn saved you from being Lady Withers' scullery maid,' Phoebe pointed out.

She didn't want him to fall on his knees and kiss Finn's feet. That would be going too far, especially with the state of Finn's socks. But a quick 'Thank you' would only be polite.

'Where is Finn, by the way?' asked Phoebe, looking round. 'I wanted to ask what he wrote in that letter to make her blow her top like that. It must have been something really rude!'

'He said he was going down to the cellar – I

think he's gone to get his cast-off spider skin,' said Miss Burgess.

Immediately Dr Clinton perked up. He became quite lively, like a puppet whose strings have been jerked. It was the word *spider* that did it.

'Where did he find this cuticle?' asked Dr Clinton. He sounded much more self-assured. He knew where he was with spiders. Spiders made him feel secure.

'Down in the caves,' Phoebe answered him immediately. 'You can get there from your cellar. Finn said it was a special find. It was *this* big,' Phoebe stretched out her hands. 'It must have come from a monster spider.'

'So it's true . . .' Dr Clinton murmured to himself with a grim look. He seemed to have forgotten to be shy and ill at ease. He'd even stopped talking to the furniture. He immediately took charge of the situation. 'I'm afraid,' he said, 'that there's something nasty down in those caves.'

'What is it, Clinton?' asked Miss Burgess. Even she sounded flustered. To her own surprise, she had a soft spot for Finn.

'There's always been a rumour in spider

circles,' said Dr Clinton, 'about Lord Withers. He had a fantastic spider collection. The story goes he had some very rare specimens. So rare that now we only find them in fossil form. But he had them *alive.*' His voice had sunk to an awed whisper.

'So what kind of spiders were they?' demanded Phoebe anxiously.

'Primitive spiders,' said Dr Clinton. 'Heaven knows where he found them. We all thought they'd died out – over 250 million years ago when modern spiders evolved. I never really believed he'd got them. And no one could prove it, because, after he disappeared, his spider collection vanished as well. No one knew what happened to it.'

But Miss Burgess could guess. She had a sudden vision in her head of The Servants' Friend flushing rare spiders down the sink – beautiful tropical spiders like tiny jewels, handsome tarantulas with soft, chestnut-coloured fur. She probably had to give *them* a good prod with a sink plunger. Flower spiders, sun spiders, violin spiders – she wouldn't care. They'd all go the same way. Down the drain.

'These primitive spiders,' Miss Burgess asked her nephew, 'could you flush them down the sink?'

'They wouldn't let you,' said Dr Clinton, with a troubled look in his eyes.

'Hang on. I thought spiders are more scared of us then we are of them,' said Phoebe.

'Not these spiders,' said Dr Clinton, looking even more haunted.

'So is Finn in danger?' asked Miss Burgess briskly. 'He should have been back by now.'

'I don't know,' admitted Dr Clinton, talking more to himself than to them. 'If Dr Withers did have these primitive spiders in his collection. If they escaped after he disappeared. If they survived down in the caves. That's a lot of 'if's. I'd have to see that cuticle. I'd have to go down there for a look.'

He started towards the door.

'We'll go with you!' said Phoebe.

'No,' Miss Burgess held her back. 'This is a job for a spider expert. He knows what he's doing. Having people around would only unsettle him.'

'Hmmm,' said Phoebe anxiously. She wasn't convinced. Someone who can only

communicate with spiders doesn't inspire your confidence.

Dr Clinton, successful spider psychologist but complete failure with people, hurried down to the cellar. His nerdy leather sandals slapped on the stone steps. He was excited. His spider-hunting instincts were aroused. But so were his fears. If it was true that primitive spiders were loose under The Lair, then he was going to need all his skills. He had only, so far, solved the problems of sophisticated, modern spiders. Psychoanalysing their primitive ancestors was going to be a different thing altogether.

The cellar was empty.

'Finn?' shouted Dr Clinton. No answer. Then he saw the shed spider skin. It was lying by the entrance to the underground caves, on top of the stone slab that Miss Burgess had man-handled out of the way.

Dr Clinton's expression grew grimmer. Where was Finn? Why hadn't he collected his find? No self-respecting spider fanatic would give up a treasure like this – not without a struggle.

Very gently, Dr Clinton picked up the exoskeleton. It was light as a bubble. It looked like a tangle of withered, contorted legs. His expert eye examined it.

'It was true all the time,' he murmured to himself. All those old stories about Lord Withers' unique spider specimens. It was the main reason he'd bought The Lair – because Lord Withers, author of *Pooter Hunting for Boys,* had once lived here. Dr Clinton hadn't given a thought to Lady Withers. He hadn't thought she was important. That was his big mistake.

'Finn?' Dr Clinton shouted.

Again no answer. Then he thought he heard something – a strangled shout in the distance. It came from the hole at his feet, the entrance to the tunnels.

Dr Clinton carefully put down the cuticle. He put both sandalled feet into the hole. The rest of his body slid after them, down, deep down into the green wavy light.

Chapter Thirteen

Waiting for Dr Clinton to come back with Finn was a nerve-wracking business. Phoebe paced up and down the gloomy library, carefully avoiding the smear of grey dust on the carpet. Hard to believe that someone with such power over people had just fizzled out like a firework. She didn't like looking at it; it was too creepy. She got a dustpan and brush from Dr Clinton's cleaning collection and, gritting her teeth, swept up The Servants' Friend.

'Shall we go for that cup of tea in the kitchen?' suggested Miss Burgess.

'Can you smell anything?' asked Phoebe as they went out the library door.

'Only the smell of scorched carpet,' said Miss Burgess firmly. 'Don't worry. She's gone for good.'

At least the kitchen was more cheerful. The copper pans gleamed. Dr Clinton's elbow grease had made everything sparkle.

Wait a minute, thought Phoebe, as Miss Burgess clattered about with tea cups. She'd remembered the copy of *Arm Oil and Elbow Grease* in her pocket – the one she'd found in the attic. She also had the photo of Lady Withers.

'So that's what she looked like,' said Miss Burgess thoughtfully, as Phoebe showed her the picture. 'Ratty little thing, isn't she? You wouldn't think she could cause all that trouble.'

Phoebe laughed with relief. She was pleased Miss Burgess was so rude about Lady Withers. Whenever she looked at the photo it made her skin crawl.

'And I found this,' said Phoebe, opening *Arm Oil and Elbow Grease* at the *Answers to Correspondents* page. 'I never got time to check. I just wondered if Ruby sent any more letters.'

She scanned the list of replies from The Servants' Friend. It was the usual mixture of fusspot advice and crushing comments.

To Maud, parlour maid.

You appear to be a shockingly vain little girl. Forget about your spots. Be quite assured no one is taking the least notice of YOU. Put mustard powder on your chilblains.

The Servants' Friend

Phoebe's heart gave a great jolt. There it was: *To Ruby Dove.* She'd hardly dared hope. Now she hardly dared read the reply. She clutched the magazine with trembling fingers.

To Ruby Dove, she read, *student servant.*

You say your dream is to be an engineer, like your father. I fear I cannot help smiling. It is such an unsuitable career for a girl! You are bound to fail. As for your other question, if you are bleeding from the lungs of course it is a serious matter! Your handwriting is quite disgraceful.

The Servants' Friend

Phoebe's head was spinning. 'You horrible, cruel old witch,' she murmured. She felt sick and dizzy. She had to sit down. She let *Arm Oil and Elbow Grease* drop from her fingers.

Miss Burgess picked up the magazine. As she read Lady Withers' reply her face grew grave.

'Oh dear,' she sighed. 'This has jogged my memory. I know where else I've seen the name Ruby Dove. It was years and years ago –'

'Where?' asked Phoebe.

'On a gravestone,' said Miss Burgess, trying to make her foghorn voice more mellow. 'I read old gravestones. It's a hobby of mine.'

'I don't want to know,' cried Phoebe hysterically, blocking her ears. 'I'm not going to listen!'

Miss Burgess sat patiently at the table until, at last, Phoebe let her hands fall from her ears.

'Have a cup of tea,' suggested Miss Burgess.

'I hate tea,' said Phoebe, pushing it away.

'I remember that gravestone now. Poor Ruby was only thirteen when she died. And from Lady Withers' reply, she'd probably got TB. Consumption, they called it then. There was no cure for it,' said Miss Burgess, shaking her head sorrowfully. 'Lots of people died of it.'

'It's not fair!' shouted Phoebe wildly.

Miss Burgess patted her awkwardly on the

arm. 'At least she escaped Lady Withers' clutches. Lady Withers wouldn't have wanted her once she got frail and sick.'

That was no comfort at all to Phoebe.

'But she died!' she cried out again in an outraged voice.

She felt, in some weird way, that Ruby had escaped from her too. Now she'd never have the chance to tell her all the things she wanted.

'I was going to be her friend! I was going to write her good advice!'

Miss Burgess looked on helplessly. 'It's very bad luck,' she said.

'Bad luck!' shouted Phoebe. 'It's not just bad luck. It's horrible. I can't stand it. I can't believe she died when she was just a kid – without ever getting her dream. It's not fair!' And she put her head down on the kitchen table and sobbed.

Miss Burgess wasn't very good with emotions. She found them a bit messy. But she suddenly had an idea. She rummaged in her backpack and came out with Philip Dove's leather-bound notebook.

'Do you want to know what Ruby Dove's dream was? *Why* she wanted to be an engineer?'

Phoebe raised her head, sniffing and red-eyed. 'What's the point of that?' she demanded. It just seemed like more grief.

Miss Burgess gave a hopeless shrug. 'It'll pass the time,' she suggested, 'until Clinton and Finn come back.'

'I told you I don't want to know!' shouted Phoebe, letting her head slump to the table again.

Miss Burgess didn't put the notebook away. She just waited, patiently . . .

Chapter Fourteen

Dr Clinton searched for Finn through the wavy green gloom of the underground tunnels.

He was still very confused about what had happened since he moved into The Lair, but he tried to clear his mind and concentrate on the job in hand. Luckily, concentrating on spiders was what he did best.

He needed his brain to be sharp for two reasons. One, you could easily get lost in this maze of caves and tunnels. And two, primitive spiders were likely to be his biggest challenge yet. They were spider relics, throwbacks to a time before dinosaurs. They should have been as dead as the dodo. He wondered where on earth Lord Withers had found them.

No, don't let your mind wander, he warned himself. He needed to stay alert.

He kept shouting down the tunnels, 'Finn! Finn!' But there was no reply. His voice just kept echoing back.

He passed through a spectacular cave. Sparkling white crystals hung from the roof in clusters like chandeliers. But there was no time to marvel. He hurried on.

He did allow himself to puzzle over two things. Why weren't these tunnels full of water? The natural springs that flowed through here must have been dammed up somewhere. And there were other signs of human interference. Those holes made in the rock, for instance. They were everywhere, all different sizes. They would make ideal dens for primitive spiders.

'Finn!' Dr Clinton called again. 'Where are you?'

He frowned. He had a chilling feeling that the longer Finn was missing, the less likely he was to be found.

Experts argued about primitive spiders. Their big, hairy bodies were sometimes found imprinted in rocks, millions of years old. But not often. Spider fossils are very rare, so most of what is known about them is guesswork.

Primitive spiders probably didn't build webs in the air. They couldn't do anything so complex. Their hunting techniques were crude. They chased their prey along the ground with big stabbing claws. They were crushers and mashers, not cunning creeper-uppers. They made modern spiders look clever.

'Oh no!'

Dr Clinton's face turned ashy grey. He'd just turned into another cave, dimmer than the rest, with strange, spindly columns twisting like candy sticks from floor to ceiling. And, in a heap among them, was a human skeleton.

Dr Clinton crept closer. His scientific brain took over. It wasn't Finn, that was for sure. This skeleton was an adult, and it had been here a very long time.

It should have been scary. But, somehow, it wasn't. The skeleton was weirdly beautiful, glittering with sparkly white jewels where water had dripped and made bone into crystal.

It's him, thought Dr Clinton with more

sadness than horror. It's my boyhood hero, Lord Withers. Poor old chap.

The biggest mystery in spider circles had finally been solved. There was no mistake. For, lying beside his bones was a personalized pooter. It was engraved with the name *WITHERS*. It was the biggest pooter Dr Clinton had ever seen. Unlike any Lord Withers had described in *Pooter Hunting for Boys*. It wasn't made of glass but of metal. It was obviously specially designed for spiders that would put up a fight.

Dr Clinton picked up the enormous pooter. It was like hefting an anti-tank gun. It was in perfect condition, made of zinc, so the big grey tube wasn't even rusty. You didn't use your lung power for this one. It had a plunger at one end to suck in the spiders, and a grille at the other, like a little portcullis, that snapped down to trap them.

He didn't want to use it. It wasn't his style. He liked to have a meeting of minds with spiders. But he had an awful suspicion that these civilized tactics weren't going to work with primitive spiders.

It was against all his principles. But he was

going to have to get tough. He gave a last salute to Lord Withers' sparkling bones. How had his hero died? There was no telling. But Dr Clinton didn't even have time to guess. He was on an urgent rescue mission. Lives were at stake.

Grasping his giant pooter, Dr Clinton plunged deeper into the tunnels.

'Finn?' No answer.

Dr Clinton had one more weapon. He was really reluctant to use it. It brought back all his childhood hang-ups. It was the main reason he was so shy and awkward with other people.

Come on, Clint! he mocked himself. You're not going to let this boy down, are you, just because you're embarrassed you're not *normal*?

Dr Clinton made a decision. He kicked off his nerdy sandals and winced as his tender soles hit the hard rock. Then, as carefully as a praying mantis moves her limbs, he lifted up one leg, wiggled his toes – and *sniffed*!

Like spiders, Dr Clinton could smell with his feet. Wearing trainers on his TV show had been torture to him. Who wants to smell their own cheesy feet all day? That was why, in

private, he always wore sandals – to get more air circulation.

Dr Clinton's parents soon found out that their baby was different. It was sniffing flowers with his feet that first made them suspicious. They swore him to secrecy. They gave him dreadful warnings: 'Other children won't play with you!' So, as a child, he'd played mostly with spiders. With them, he didn't feel like a freak.

His feet had been a big family secret all these years. Ever since his parents had died. No one else knew about them. Except, of course, Aunt Flossie.

What's that I smell? thought Dr Clinton, cocking his leg sideways like a dog at a lamp post and snuffling hard.

Doctor Clinton could smell through his nose too. But his feet were super-sensitive sniffers. They could pick up a human smell from half a kilometre away. They could probably sniff Finn's smell from even further, especially if this wasn't the week he changed his socks.

Phew! thought Dr Clinton, his feet crinkling up in disgust. Never mind, he'd found the trail.

He gripped his giant-size pooter even more grimly, like a soldier going into battle.

Treading gingerly over the rocks, stopping to wave a leg in the air every now and then to search for smells, he started tracking Finn down.

Chapter Fifteen

'Philip Dove was a genius, of course,' said Miss Burgess. 'He was far ahead of his time.'

She was talking to the top of Phoebe's head. Phoebe was still slumped over the kitchen table, her hot, tear-stained face resting on her arms. Her eyes were closed. It seemed like she'd fallen asleep.

But when Miss Burgess added, 'Then his life's work was ruined by Lady Withers,' Phoebe's eyes snapped open. Her head shot up.

'Did she give him rubbish advice too?' asked Phoebe angrily. How many people's lives had that woman wrecked?

'Not exactly,' said Miss Burgess. 'At first she had nothing to do with him. Philip Dove was working for Lord Withers. They had a grand engineering scheme for the garden of The Lair. Philip Dove used this notebook to write down his plans. Look, here's a drawing of an engine that was meant to pump water through the tunnels.'

Miss Burgess flashed Phoebe a picture of valves and plungers and twisting pipes. 'What a wonderful machine! It still exists, you know, Phoebe – in the old pump house out in the garden.'

Phoebe's head drooped again. She could skip this bit. People meant more to her than machines. She would start listening again when Ruby Dove got involved.

'Anyway,' said Miss Burgess hastily, seeing that Phoebe's attention was drifting, 'to cut a long story short, the very day Lord Withers disappeared, Lady Withers sacked Ruby Dove's father. He wasn't allowed down the tunnels again. Plus, there was money owing to him that she never paid. Quite a lot of money.'

'What did she sack him for?' asked Phoebe, her head springing up again at the mention of Ruby's name. 'Wasn't he going to make the rock garden beautiful?'

'The Servants' Friend wasn't interested in beautiful,' said Miss Burgess. 'She was only interested in useful. And besides, Philip Dove's dreams for the garden didn't involve dusting.'

'Did she *deliberately* ruin him?' interrupted Phoebe.

'Oh yes, I should think so,' replied Miss Burgess matter-of-factly. 'Out of sheer spite probably. It would be just her style, wouldn't it? He had a dream, you see. She was always jealous of people with dreams.'

'So what happened to him and Ruby?' Phoebe was curious again now. In any case, asking questions stopped her worrying about what was happening to Finn.

'It's a bit upsetting I'm afraid,' warned Miss Burgess.

But Phoebe held her head up. She'd cried all she was going to cry. She'd cried buckets. There were no more tears left.

'Because he wasn't paid,' Miss Burgess went on, 'he couldn't pay all his debts. He and Ruby ended up in the workhouse. He didn't last long in there. He seems to have wasted away. Died of a broken heart. Ruby had no other relations. She only had her dad – her mum seems to have died when she was a baby. So she got sent to an orphanage, then to Servants' School.

'How do you know all this?' asked Phoebe.

'Ruby told me.'

Miss Burgess saw Phoebe's face brighten with hope, so she added hastily, 'In the notebook, I mean. Didn't you read all the notes she scribbled in the margins?'

Phoebe shook her head. 'Only some stuff she wrote about her dad's machines.'

'Well, she wrote other things too. About her dad and how much she missed him. And about her dream. It was Ruby's dream to become an engineer, like her dad, and to finish his life's work.'

Miss Burgess felt a personal interest in Ruby Dove. Two important things linked them – muscles and machines. Miss Burgess had a lonely childhood, with only wild moorland sheep to play with. If Ruby Dove had been around she knew they would have been friends. She was as upset as Phoebe over Ruby Dove's tragic early death, although she found it much harder to show it.

But there was something else she *could* do.

‘Poor Ruby never got the chance. But we could do it,’ Miss Burgess suggested, in a sudden rush of words.

‘What did you say?’ asked Phoebe. She didn’t quite catch it. Miss Burgess had sounded nervous. That surprised Phoebe because Miss Burgess wasn’t the nervous type.

‘We could finish Philip Dove’s grand scheme,’ Miss Burgess explained. ‘I’ve been thinking about it. It wouldn’t be impossible. All the machinery’s still here.’

‘No!’ Phoebe interrupted forcefully. She couldn’t face it. She didn’t want all that grief stirred up again. She didn’t want anything to do with history. Miss Burgess was right – no good came from meddling with it.

‘No,’ she insisted again, ‘Ruby’s dead, her dad’s dead –’

‘You mean, let them both rest?’ Miss Burgess finished the sentence for her. Then she gave an understanding nod. ‘Perhaps you’re right,’ she said, shutting Philip Dove’s notebook away in her backpack.

Chapter Sixteen

Dr Clinton's sniffer feet were stalking Finn's smell through the tunnels. But an alarming thing had just happened. Dr Clinton was being stalked himself.

He knew it as soon as the hairs on the back of his neck started tingling. Then he heard a scrabbling sound. He had heard that before, when tarantulas scraped their claws against rocks. But this was much, much louder.

He came out into another light-dappled cave. The map in his head of the way back was getting complicated now – he had taken so many twists and turns. But he knew he was getting very close to Finn. He could be just round the corner. That smell of hair gel, cheesy feet and human meat was really strong now.

He shifted his pooter under his left arm. He would only use it as a last resort, if psychology failed.

Suddenly there was the *wubbering* sound of wild beating wings. He ducked. A bat zig-zagged across the cave. It nearly parted his hair! From one of the neatly drilled holes halfway up the cave wall hurtled a large, hairy torpedo. It snatched the bat in mid-air, then dropped to the floor and scuttled behind a rock to suck out its insides.

'Oh dear,' said Dr Clinton.

He knew primitive spiders were big.

He guessed they were fast.

But he didn't know they could jump.

'I'm here!' came a feeble voice.

Dr Clinton's eyes searched the cave. They found Finn pinned to the wall by hundreds of sticky strands of spider silk. Only his head was free.

'They haven't eaten me yet,' said Finn, stating the obvious. 'I think they're saving me until later.'

Finn was so relieved to see his hero, he thought all his problems were over. He even forgot to be terrified. 'It's dead interesting, isn't it?' he said, almost chattily, to Dr Clinton. 'In *Pooter Hunting for Boys* it says spiders are solitary creatures. But this lot aren't. These primitive spiders hunt in packs.'

'Oh dear,' said Dr Clinton again.

At that precise moment, he became aware of a forest of strange, pale eyes all around him. They glittered like pearls from the holes Philip Dove had so carefully drilled as part of his grand scheme. How was he to know they'd make perfect primitive-spider burrows?

A bunch of legs as thick as bananas shuffled out of one hole. A brown furry body squeezed after, then sprang like a wolf to the cave floor.

For the first time, Dr Clinton had a clear view of a primitive, bat-eating spider. It was about knee-height, raised up on its eight hairy legs. It had two milky eyes. They were small and squinty, but eyes aren't much use in the near darkness. It made up for them with poisonous fangs and two deadly stabbing claws.

It raised itself even higher like a cat ready to pounce. It rubbed its front legs together. They made an angry buzzing sound.

'Watch out!'cried Finn, still glued to the wall. 'It's going to attack!'

'Shhh,' said Dr Clinton. He was trying to keep his brain icy cool.

In all his spider experience, Dr Clinton had never seen a more aggressive specimen. Could he calm it down? Even win its trust, as he'd done with hundreds of modern spiders on his own TV show?

Very, very carefully, so as not to startle it, Dr Clinton laid down the pooter. He was an expert in spider communication.

He raised his right arm and waggled it slowly. Then his left. That meant, in modern spider speak, 'I am approaching your web. Don't eat me.'

The cobra-like hissing continued.

Dr Clinton tried another tactic. It always worked on modern spiders. He started rubbing his own legs together. Spiders don't have ears, but they can sense vibration. The rough denim of Dr Clinton's jeans produced the perfect spider-soothing sound. He'd tried on sixty-two pairs of jeans before he'd found the right ones. He'd been thrown out of three shops – stridulating in changing rooms makes shop assistants suspicious.

So that's why he always wears tight jeans,

thought Finn, highly impressed. And I just thought he had no fashion sense! He should have known better. Finn's admiration for his hero was increasing by the second.

Finn's faith in his hero might have been sky-high, but Dr Clinton was seriously rattled. How could he get through to this primitive spider? None of his usual methods worked. Compared to modern spiders it was a complete brute. It hadn't even evolved enough to have a language.

This is useless, thought Dr Clinton. He stopped trying to make conversation. The primitive spider's tiny eyes watched him. They seemed to wink in the dim light. But there was no understanding in them.

Reluctantly, Dr Clinton picked up the pooter. With a war-like glint in his eyes, he aimed it at the spider.

'Who's a pretty boy then?' said Dr Clinton, pushing in the plunger of the pooter. 'Come and see what I've got for you.'

The spider gathered in its legs. A furry blur launched itself at Dr Clinton. One bite from those dripping fangs would mean death.

Dr Clinton caught it in mid-air. The spider

never knew what hit it. Dr Clinton drew back the plunger and, *whoosh*, the flying arachnid was sucked right in. The grille clanged down. It was trapped.

'Yay!' yelled Finn, as if he was already saved. 'That showed 'em!'

Dr Clinton knew different. He put down the heavy pooter. His arms were aching badly. The other primitive spiders were already swarming down the cave walls.

There was only one thing for it.

'*Run!*' he shouted to Finn, exploding into action. Darting across the cave floor, he ripped Finn free of his sticky bonds. He grabbed his arm. 'Come on!'

Primitive spiders aren't famous for being quick-thinking. It took them five minutes to realize their prey was making a run for it. That gave Finn and Dr Clinton a good head start.

Dr Clinton's sensitive sniffer feet were smarting. But he never even felt the pain. He and Finn ran as if a pack of demons were after them. The primitive spiders hadn't learned much. They couldn't spin webs that were works of art or speak spider language, but they were mean hunting machines.

'Down here!' yelled Dr Clinton, dragging Finn the right way.

Behind them, a long-legged gang of furry killers was closing in fast. They didn't make much noise as they chased their prey. Just scratchings and scrabblings. Some scuttled. Some gave great silent, springy leaps like velociraptors.

Their greedy eyes gleamed with one purpose. Bats are tough and leathery. It gets boring eating them day in, day out, year in, year out. Besides, they're only snack-sized. They hadn't sucked the insides out of anything big and soft and squishy for a long, long time.

Lord Withers' bones sparkled in the gloom as Dr Clinton and Finn raced past. Did Finn know what they were? It was hard to tell, all covered with crystals like that. Did he even see them? He gave no sign. But Dr Clinton caught a flashing glimpse of something he'd missed before. It looked like a huge, cobwebby ball stuck to the cave roof. It was jerking and wriggling. Bulges kept popping up on its surface. Whatever was inside was trying to get out.

'They're breeding!' gasped Dr Clinton as a primitive spiderling, the size of a fist, chewed its way out of the egg sac.

They barely made it back. Dr Clinton hauled Finn out of the tunnels on to the cellar floor.

'Quick!' he panted. 'Or they'll catch us!'

It took two of them to shift the stone slab that Miss Burgess had moved so easily. It was only halfway across when two hairy legs came groping out. The legs shot back as, with a heave and a grunt, Finn and Dr Clinton slid the slab into place.

'That'll hold 'em,' said Finn.

Dr Clinton thought so too – until the slab began wobbling. The crush of primitive spiders beneath it was forcing it upwards. They didn't like being deprived of their dinner . . .

Chapter Seventeen

Finn and Dr Clinton staggered into the kitchen.

'They're trying to get out!' shrieked Finn. His eyes were wild and haunted, his face deathly pale. Silvery shreds of spider thread fluttered from his clothes and hair. He looked like a tattered ghost.

'Finn!' said Phoebe. She was thrilled he was back safe. 'What happened?'

'I just got kidnapped by *completely uncivilized spiders*!' babbled Finn. 'And stuck to the wall! They wanted to have me for dinner!'

'Eh?' said Phoebe.

Dr Clinton took over the explanation. Obviously Finn still hadn't got over the shock. His encounters with spiders previously had been peaceful and friendly. He wasn't used to spiders who made your stress levels soar.

'There are primitive spiders down in the tunnels,' Dr Clinton said briefly. 'A big colony of them. And they're trying to get out.'

'Did you put back the stone slab?' asked Miss Burgess equally briskly. She was great in a crisis. It brought out the best in her.

Dr Clinton nodded. 'But that's not going to stop them. Some of those holes lead right up to the stone garden. They've smelled humans. They're not going to stay down there and eat bats.'

Dr Clinton didn't tell them about Lord Withers' jewelled bones. There wasn't the time. Some modern spiders live for forty years. But what if these ancient spiders lived longer than that? What if some of them dimly remembered the taste of humans from way back – when they'd made a meal of poor Lord Withers?

'There'll be no stopping them once they get out,' said Dr Clinton grimly. 'There'll be mass panic.'

'That's right!' raved Finn, his hair and clothes still sparkling with shiny strands, like a

Christmas tree loaded with tinsel. 'Fancy finding one of them under your bed! My mum goes mad if she finds an itty-bitty spider. And these are –' Finn stretched out his arms, 'that big! You'd have a job flushing them down the toilet!'

'Not down the toilet,' said Miss Burgess thoughtfully. 'But you could flush them through the tunnels. I mean, you could drown them.' She looked across at Phoebe, as if they shared a secret.

'Philip Dove's pumping engine!' said Phoebe, her brain finally coming up for some fresh air from the depths of despair. 'Will it still work?'

'I don't know,' said Miss Burgess.

Dr Clinton gave a puzzled look from one to the other. He knew about spiders. But this was about Ruby Dove and her dad. This was where Phoebe and Miss Burgess were experts.

'If we're right,' explained Miss Burgess, 'we should be able to flood every cave and tunnel down there with water.' She'd already got Philip's Dove's notebook out of her backpack and was busy consulting it. 'I'll need the keys to the pump house,' she said.

'You know where they'll be,' said Phoebe. 'On *her* bunch of keys, in the library.'

For the first time, Phoebe thanked her lucky stars that The Servants' Friend. was such a control freak and fusspot, with a place for everything and everything in its place.

'Come on!' boomed Miss Burgess. 'If what you say about these spiders is true then there's no time to lose.'

Dr Clinton hesitated. It went against all his instincts, as a scholar and a spider lover, to wipe out arachnids. Especially a species that should have died out before dinosaurs. What about all the scientists who'd be queuing up to study them?

'Can't we save one or two?' he started to ask. In his career as a spider psychologist he'd come across plenty of arachnids with bad attitudes. Perhaps, in time, he could persuade even primitive spiders to become perfect pets.

'No way!' cried Finn, appalled. Those fiendish spiders had scooted up out of nowhere. They'd herded him to their underground larder, where they kept their prey fresh until they fancied turning its insides to mush. It made his flesh crawl recalling their white wolfish eyes and raptors' fangs.

'They should be fossils!' cried Finn. 'They don't belong on earth any more!'

Dr Clinton shrugged sadly. He knew it made sense. Primitive spiders should have died out. Where had Lord Withers found these few survivors? In an extinct volcano in Peru? In a prehistoric cave in Africa? He should have left them there. They were deadly dangerous. They'd scoff anything they could get their claws on.

Finn's right, thought Dr Clinton. People went crazy when cute little spiderlings the size of a pinhead came abseiling down from the ceiling. How would they cope with an invasion of primitive spiders colonizing the sewers, lifting up drain covers in high streets and scanning Saturday shoppers for the plumpest, juiciest prey? It would be like those wildlife programmes on telly, where lions run down lumbering water buffalo.

'Nightmare!' decided Dr Clinton, shuddering.

'Stop dithering, Clinton!' commanded Miss Burgess sternly. 'Stop thinking and get moving!' The sooner they got Philip Dove's pumping engine started the better.

Phoebe dashed into the library as they passed and snatched Lady Withers' keys. She deliberately didn't look at the dustpan.

'Catch you up,' said Dr Clinton, suddenly remembering his tender sniffer feet. They'd be torn to shreds by the rocks in the garden. 'I must put some shoes on.'

No one stopped to ask where he'd left his sandals. Phoebe, Finn and Miss Burgess were too busy hurrying outside. As they scrambled over crags, Finn checked every drill hole. No sign yet of spiders swarming up from the depths. They were probably still trying to batter their way through the stone slab. It would take their simple brains some time to work out that there were other, much easier, exits.

Miss Burgess powered far ahead, her tweedy skirt swinging, her hair like an orange sunburst.

Phoebe felt brave with Miss Burgess. Was it because of the sheep wrestling? Wrestling sheep and wrestling spiders isn't quite the same thing. Spiders have got twice as many legs for a start. But Miss Burgess looked like she could rip them apart with her bare hands.

Finn wasn't so confident. He'd seen these throwback arachnids and Phoebe hadn't. He'd looked right into their primeval eyes. And he knew that even Miss Burgess was no match for them.

Miss Burgess waited patiently while Phoebe fitted key after key into the pump-house door.

'That one!' she cried, yanking open the door. 'I knew that old witch would have it!'

'Well, well, well,' said Miss Burgess as they got their first good look at what was inside. She needn't have worried. She'd been afraid that Philip Dove's water-pumping machine would be rusted up, impossible to start after 120 years.

'Have you been polishing down here?' she demanded as Dr Clinton appeared in the doorway. He was wearing *trainers*, but this was an emergency. Putting up with the smell of his own feet was a small price to pay.

Dr Clinton looked around, puzzled. 'I can't remember,' he said. Thankfully, his days spent as scullery maid and chief polisher for The Servants' Friend were a total blank.

But someone had put in a lot of elbow grease. The valves and plungers and pistons were gleaming and well oiled. The machinery was spotless. Like the engine of a brand new car.

'Quite amazing,' said Miss Burgess, peering into the machinery. 'Look! Look!' she roared, pointing. 'There's a bronze double-beat poppet valve! You don't often see them!' She sounded thrilled to bits.

Dr Clinton coughed politely, '*Err,* Aunt Flossie. We're supposed to be saving the world. Remember? From savage spiders? Who can suck out your insides?'

'Like vampires,' added Finn.

'Sorry,' said Miss Burgess, embarrassed. 'I got carried away.'

'How's it work?' asked Finn. It looked like a load of scrap metal to him.

'Simple,' said Miss Burgess. 'It's all done with water power. Water drives the pump engine. Then the engine blasts the water at great pressure through the caves and tunnels. Those vampire spiders won't stand a chance. Only problem is,' said Miss Burgess, looking round frowning, 'where's the water?'

She flicked through Philip Dove's notebook.

Then her face lit up with understanding. 'The crafty beggar,' she marvelled. Miss Burgess sprang to a large iron wheel in the corner. 'He dammed up an underground stream,' she explained. 'There are big wooden gates down there holding back the water. Turning this wheel opens the gates, lets the streams flow and, hey presto, the whole caboodle should start running. Of course, that's theoretical,' admitted Miss Burgess, 'because Philip Dove never got the chance to test it.'

'Now's the time, Auntie,' said Dr Clinton, rushing to look out of the pump-house door. 'The first spider's worked out how to get up here.'

'Keep it back, Clinton!' thundered Miss Burgess. 'I repeat, don't let it out of the tunnels! Come on, Phoebe, let's turn this wheel.'

Finn dashed out after Dr Clinton, with silky threads fluttering like fringes all over him.

Dr Clinton was staring down into a hole. Two furry legs were already creeping out, exploring the edge. Two more followed.

'We need something to poke it back down with!' yelled Finn.

Where was the titanium hiking stick and tea

cup when you needed it? Then he remembered. It hadn't stood up to Miss Burgess's muscles. It was down in the cellar, curled into a 'C' shape.

There was a leg lying about – another body part belonging to one of the crumbling statues. Desperately, Finn grabbed it. He jabbed it down the hole. Two beady white eyes peered back at him. Like lightning, the leg was whipped from his grasp. Strong spider claws crunched it to chalky fragments.

Oh no, thought Finn, I've made it mad now!

The primitive spider hauled itself to the surface and squatted, like a big hairy toad, on the rock. Its tiny eyes watched Finn. It wasn't in a hurry. It knew he couldn't escape. It was just wondering when to jump.

'Run!' Finn's brain shrieked at him.

'Don't move,' warned Dr Clinton. 'It'll chase you.'

He sounded cool. Just like he did on his TV show when he was confident of solving a spider's problems.

Very, very carefully, with his eyes all the time on the spider, he took off his trainers.

*

Inside the pump house, Phoebe and Miss Burgess were struggling to turn the wheel. But it wouldn't budge. The iron spokes hurt your hands. Whatever it was connected to deep underground seemed to be jammed.

'I can't shift it!' puffed Miss Burgess.

Phoebe couldn't help wishing that Ruby Dove had been here. The three of them would have made a good team. She could almost see Ruby, pasty-faced in her Servants' School frock and clumpy boots. But her eyes would have been shining, because she'd be getting her dad's machinery up and running again.

'We're trying, Ruby,' whispered Phoebe.

Miss Burgess put her shoulder against the wheel.

'We need Ruby's muscles!' said Phoebe. Miss Burgess nodded, then gave an extra-hard shove. The wheel jolted forward. From underground came a wrenching crack. Then a very faint gurgling sound.

'Water!' cried Miss Burgess. 'The dam gates are opening. Push harder!'

Out in the stone garden, the primitive spider had decided to make a move. It was raising

itself up on its long legs. Its tiny eyes glittered.

No point trying to outrun it, thought Dr Clinton. It could sprint as fast as a cheetah.

'Copy me!' he cried urgently to Finn. 'It's our only chance!'

Dr Clinton raised his arms high, then began to move them slowly from side to side as if he was part of a Mexican wave. He needn't have taken off his trainers for this, but it got him in the mood.

'What are you doing?' said Finn, open-mouthed. Had his hero cracked under the strain?

'I'm pretending to be a female spider, of course!' hissed Dr Clinton. 'I'm sending out threatening display signals. *Don't approach! I'm not feeling romantic. I am going to attack!*'

Dr Clinton might not know much about getting girlfriends. But he was red-hot on mating rituals in spiders.

'Copy me!' insisted Dr Clinton.

Female spiders are not lovey-dovey. Their mates often end up as their next meal.

'Now I'm getting really menacing!' warned Dr Clinton.

He began to vibrate his whole body

violently, while still waving his arms slowly from side to side. It was a spectacular performance. He looked as if he was shaking himself to bits.

'Wow!' said Finn, impressed.

He started doing the arm-waving. But that body-wobbling bit was beyond him. You'd have to have practised a lot to do that.

The primitive spider was convinced. Because he was so dim and had such weak eyesight he saw two furious leg-waving females. 'You're outnumbered!' his simple brain told him.

Male spiders don't mess with one female spider. And never, ever, with two. Not if they want to stay alive. He shuffled quickly backwards down his hole.

'It won't work for long!' said Dr Clinton, putting the brake on his body quivering. Finn was quite surprised to see his hero still in one piece.

'Look!' said Finn, lowering his arms and pointing a horrified finger.

More primitive spiders had sneaked to the surface. All around them, legs were furtively feeling their way out of holes.

We might as well say our prayers, thought

Dr Clinton. He'd done all he could, but it wasn't enough. The primitive spiders were going to wreak havoc among unsuspecting humans.

But not if Miss Burgess could help it. Exhausted, she and Phoebe stopped turning the wheel. The underground stream was flowing freely now. Water was gushing through the pipes of the pump engine. Was it going to work, after all this time? Like a great metal monster coming to life, it suddenly began juddering. The big pistons started clanking importantly. The tiny bronze double-beat poppet valves were whirring like butterflies' wings.

'It's working!' boomed Miss Burgess excitedly. Ruby would have been proud. 'It should be pumping water through the tunnels soon. Look out into the garden!'

They dashed to the pump-house door. Dr Clinton and Finn had been ambushed. From every hole in the rock around them poked a wolfish eye or vicious claw. The spider pack was preparing to close in. Dr Clinton was still desperately doing his female-spider impersonations. But he knew it was no use.

Even primitive spiders weren't daft enough to fall for his act for longer than a few minutes.

From under the stone garden came an ominous rumbling. The ground seemed to tremble. Then, *whoosh,* out of every spider hole blasted high jets of water. Finn and Dr Clinton were suddenly surrounded by fountains. On top of each tower of spray danced a primitive spider. The water seemed to be juggling them. Then, with a greedy *slurp,* it sucked them back down underground to join the raging torrent that ripped through the underground caves and tunnels, pumped by Philip Dove's marvellous machine.

Even primitive spiders couldn't survive that. It was clear that the whole colony would soon be wiped out.

The fountains gushed up again like giant geysers. This time, there were no primitive spiders bobbing about on their bubbling tops. Not a single one.

Dr Clinton couldn't resist a sigh. He was sorry, especially for the spiderlings. Like Finn, he had a soft spot for spiderlings. To break out your egg sac one minute only to be lost in swirling underground floods the next – that was too bad.

But Finn had no regrets.

'Yay! We're safe!' he cheered. He would stick with modern spiders in future. They were more cuddly, easier to make friends with. And they were more scared of you than you were of them.

'It's over,' agreed Dr Clinton.

But they'd forgotten Philip Dove's grand scheme. When they'd set his machine in motion, all they'd needed was a kind of big toilet flush to rid the world of primitive spiders. But they were going to get much, much more than that.

'Listen!' said Miss Burgess, who'd studied Philip Dove's notebook and knew what came next.

Strange noises suddenly filled the garden.

'They're coming from under my feet!' said Finn.

All the holes Philip Dove had drilled were like musical instruments meant to be played by water. Each made its own special sound as the underground flood rushed through them. Some fluted like penny whistles or boomed like didgeridoos. Some chirruped like birdcallers. Some made ringing, bell-like notes.

'Rock music!' said Phoebe, astonished.

'I told you,' said Miss Burgess, as the stone garden came alive with tunes and fountains. Even The Lair, clinging to its crag in the background, didn't look half so grim.

'What a show!' said Phoebe, stunned by the eerie sounds and sunlit spray all around her. Instead of spiders, rainbows danced on the fountain tops.

'This was Ruby Dove's dream,' said Miss Burgess. 'She wanted to get all this working.' As an ambition, it knocked the spots off dusting.

'The statues are turning!' cried Dr Clinton.

It was another of Philip Dove's amazing water-powered mechanisms. Stone grated on stone as the six statues revolved on their bases to the rock music. They were supposed to be doing a graceful dance, which is hard when you've got so many bits missing – noses, ears, limbs, even heads. As the water roared through the tunnels and the fountains splashed and the underground orchestra trilled and

boomed, the marble ladies twirled faster and faster.

'Aaaargh!' shrieked Finn, hurling himself to the ground as a head was whipped clean off. Bouncing like a football it smashed a neat hole through one of the leaded windows of The Lair.

Those statutes were out of control. They were spinning as fast as car-wash brushes!

'Duck!' yelled Dr Clinton as a stone hand scythed through the air like a death star.

'Too much water pressure!' thundered Miss Burgess as a flying finger nearly poked her eye out. 'We've got to shut down the system!'

In a hail of body parts, she and Phoebe dashed into the pump house. They wrestled the great wheel anti-clockwise. Deep under the rock they could hear the dam gates rumbling shut.

'Phew!' said Phoebe, wiping her forehead. 'Are they supposed to go that fast?'

'There are bound to be some minor hitches,' said Miss Burgess, already tinkering with the engine. 'What do you expect, after a hundred and twenty years?'

The garden seemed strangely silent when

they went back out there. In a flurry of final *tweets* the music stopped. The fountains slowed to a dribble. Soon they dried up altogether. The poor wrecked dancers wobbled to a halt. *Ping,* the last ear, like a white sea shell, snapped off and tinkled on to the rock.

'*Wow!*' said Phoebe, looking around, the rock music still ringing in her ears, her eyes still dazzled by glittering fountains. 'I wish Ruby could have seen it.'

The genius of Philip Dove had turned The Lair into a joyous carnival, instead of the dead and dusted place ruled over by Lady Withers. Against all the odds, thought Phoebe, Ruby and her dad had won, in the end.

'We'll do it again,' promised Miss Burgess. 'After I've made a few adjustments. We'll fix those statues. And next time, it'll be perfect.'

'What happened to Lord Withers' personalized pooter?' asked Finn.

Dr Clinton started to '*Um*' and '*Er*' awkwardly, as he usually did off-camera when dealing with real people.

'It's OK, I know he's dead,' said Finn, trying to help him out. 'I saw his skeleton on the way in. '

'Yes, it's very sad,' mumbled Dr Clinton. He seemed to be speaking to a rock.

'Oh, I don't know,' said Finn cheerily. 'It's the way he would have chosen to go. I bet those primitive spiders somehow escaped from his collection and he was trying to get them back. Do you think they killed him?'

'I'm not sure,' Dr Clinton answered the rock uneasily. 'It's hard to tell just from bones.'

'Even if they did,' said Phoebe, who was listening in on the conversation, 'I think *she* trapped him down there somehow. She didn't approve of spiders. She thought they made the place messy.'

'I wish I had his pooter to remember him by,' wailed Finn.

Dr Clinton wished that too. But it would be bashed to bits against the rock walls by now, along with the primitive spider inside it. Dr Clinton frowned. He was thinking boffin thoughts.

'That spider deserves a proper scientific name,' he told Phoebe and Finn. He gave it some more thought. 'What about *Vampyrolycosa Diabolis*?' he said, finally.

'Eh?' said Finn. 'What's that mean?'

'It means, Vampire Wolf Spider from Hell.'

'That's a good name,' agreed Finn.

'It's a reminder,' said Dr Clinton solemnly, 'of what a terrifying species they once were. Just in case we forget now they're all dead.'

In fact, Lord Withers' pooter was stronger than they thought. It had survived the underground flood. It had sailed on top like a little Noah's ark. Through a maze of tunnels, it floated far away from The Lair and the stone garden. It met an underground spring that carried it even further.

When the spring bubbled into the daylight, the pooter shot up with it. Now it was cruising along in a wide, slow stream. Safe in his metal lifeboat, the last living *Vampyrolycosa Diabolis* on earth wasn't worried. He didn't have the brains to be lonely, or scared. He had no idea Dr Clinton had just given him such a posh name. He peered out, his tiny pearly eyes taking in the scenery. The pooter bumped against a bank. A black rat, looking for a free ride, slithered in through the grille. It didn't slither out again. It made a change from bats.

The spider cleaned his fangs with two hairy front legs as thick as your arm. He had a dark little den, and dinner that came walking in through his own front door. He didn't have a thing in the world to complain about.

Chapter Eighteen

'Dr Clinton's getting married,' Phoebe told Ruby Dove.

Sometimes, when she took a short cut through the village churchyard, she would sit on Ruby Dove's gravestone and bring her up to date with the news. Other kids might think that was weird, but Phoebe didn't. She had always thought of Ruby Dove as a friend.

'It was love at first sight,' explained Phoebe. 'She's a lady spider expert who's fancied him for ages. Miss Burgess persuaded him to invite her out on a date.'

That had been a tricky situation. Dr Clinton had been a bag of nerves.

'She's not going to eat you!' Phoebe had said. But Dr Clinton hadn't looked convinced.

To everyone's surprise they'd hit it off. She didn't even say '*Gross!*' when Dr Clinton confessed about his spider-like sniffer feet. As far as she was concerned, that was a big plus. It made him even more attractive.

Dr Clinton had improved no end since he'd fallen in love. He'd stopped talking to furniture. In fact, he'd become quite sociable.

'There are going to be big celebrations at The Lair,' Phoebe told Ruby. 'Fountains and your dad's rock music and even fireworks! We're all going to the wedding, me and Finn and Miss Burgess and Mum and Dad.'

There'd be no hitches this time. They'd collected the body bits from the statues and stuck them back on. Apart from a nose here and a leg there, they looked perfect. Miss Burgess had fixed the machinery so the statues spun at a slow, stately place.

'Wouldn't it be marvellous,' she'd told Phoebe excitedly, 'if on the Big Day, I could get the rocks to play the wedding march. You know, '*Tum, tum, ti-tum. Tum, tum, ti-tum . . .*' She was still working on that one. It was more complicated than she thought.

'And the bride is going to have a dress all

embroidered with spiders,' said Phoebe, making a face. 'I think that's going a bit far if you ask me.'

'Oh, and I forgot to tell you,' added Phoebe. 'Finn found his zebra spider!'

Finn had never given up looking. Two weeks after The Servants' Friend had gone up in smoke, he'd been out on the moors and had found the matchbox – battered and a bit faded, but still closed. His hands had trembled as he opened it. He thought he'd find a poor, shrivelled corpse inside. But he shouldn't have under-estimated the toughness of spiders.

The zebra spider came scurrying out over his hand.

'You're alive!' Finn's face lit up with smiles.

But there was something else left inside. Puzzled, Finn shook the box. A whole crowd of tiny spiderlings came shimmering out, each on its personal silvery safety line.

'Bye!' cried Finn as they bungee-jumped to freedom. Who knows where they'd end up? They could cross the Atlantic. They could sail so high in the sky you could see them from aeroplane windows.

'Congratulations!' Finn told his zebra spider. 'I never knew you were going to be a mum!'

But she was sick of being cooped up in a matchbox with sixty-two of her kids. She was already abseiling down from his hand. She felt like killing a few flies.

Phoebe got up from the gravestone.

'Oh, and another thing I forgot,' said Phoebe. She hadn't forgotten really, she'd just left it until last. 'Miss Burgess has put a big brass plaque on the pump-house wall. It says, IN MEMORY OF RUBY AND PHILIP DOVE, ENGINEERS.'

Phoebe knew Ruby would love that, if she was listening.

Phoebe wandered out of the churchyard. Finn just happened to be passing. He had Lord Withers' *Pooter Hunting for Boys* under his arm. He was obviously out looking for spiders.

'Hey, Finn!' shouted Phoebe. She hurried after him.

'I've been to see Miss Burgess,' he said. 'She's got a new titanium hiking stick. A better one than last time.'

'Can you collapse it into a tea cup?'

'Of course not!' said Finn, as if she'd asked a really stupid question. 'But you can extend it into a clothes prop, in case you want to dry your hiking shorts after you've waded through a river. Anyway,' said Finn, changing the subject, 'did I ever tell you that Dr Clinton can smell with his feet?'

'Yes, about a million times,' said Phoebe.

'I wish I had one of my senses in the wrong place,' said Finn earnestly. 'You know, I could hear with my elbow. See out my belly button or something. It'd be cool, wouldn't it? Did I ever tell you that butterflies can taste through their feet?'

'Frequently,' sighed Phoebe.

'Or about that frog that got found with its eyes in its mouth? Actually, I wouldn't want that,' Finn decided, 'because if you wanted to see where you were going, you'd have to keep your gob open all the time, wouldn't you? Like this –' Finn opened his mouth alarmingly wide. You could see his breakfast Crispy Wheaty Pops stuck in his back teeth. 'And as soon as you closed it,' Finn blundered blindly about, 'you'd bump into everything.'

'Finn,' said Phoebe, after they'd walked a few steps in silence, 'there's one thing I've been meaning to ask you.'

'Oh yeah?' said Finn warily. Had she found out he'd raided the freezer and eaten that two-litre tub of chocolate ice cream? Or that he'd used up her giant glue stick making a spider's den?

'You know that letter you wrote to Lady Withers?' began Phoebe.

Finn breathed a sigh of relief. His secrets were safe, so far.

'The one that made her spontaneously combust?' continued Phoebe. 'Well, what did you write in it? I mean, you must have really shocked her.'

Finn looked coy. 'I did,' he admitted. 'For a start I tried to do terrible spelling and handwriting. Actually, I didn't have to try very hard to do that. But what made her blazing mad was the question I asked her.'

'What question?'

'Well,' said Finn eagerly, 'you know when I want to really embarrass Dad, I say, "Hey Dad, how do a mummy and a daddy make babies?"'

'You didn't ask her that?'

'No!' said Finn indignantly. 'What do you think I am? I asked her something a million times ruder than *that.* Plus, I put in a few jokes from *My Very, Very Rude Joke Book.* I don't think she had much of a sense of humour –'

'I'm proud of you, Finn,' interrupted Phoebe. 'You saved us all from a lifetime of dusting.'

'I know. I'm a genius,' said Finn modestly.

Chapter Nineteen

Water World was heaving with children. They were shrieking and splashing about in the pools. They were shooting down water slides in clouds of spray.

'What's that?' someone said, as a strange metal object floated into the middle of a crowd of kids.

They didn't know it, of course, but it was Lord Withers' personalized pooter. For many months, the primitive spider had been having adventures. It was like being on a holiday cruise. He'd travelled the water systems of Great Britain, through streams and sewers, through ditches and drains. And there had always been a handy supply of food. He quite liked newts and frogs. Ducklings were delicious. But he was a growing spider. And he was ready for something bigger.

Somehow his little floating home had found its way into this open-air seaside attraction, full of happy holiday-makers. A child peered through the grille.

'There's something in there.'

Quickly, *Vampyrolycosa Diabolis* drew in its legs. Its tiny eyes no longer looked gormless. They looked shifty. Travel had broadened its mind – it seemed to be evolving at a rapid rate.

'I don't know what it is,' said the child. 'It looks like – a hairy rugby ball.'

'Can you get it out?'

'I don't know,' said the child, lifting the pooter on to the pool side. 'Hang on. I think you can undo this grille . . .'